Cover Copy

There can be only one…for both of them.

Fae-blooded Layla holds a fearsome battle skill, the 'power of thought.' She can levitate, move objects and people, and all with only a thought from her mind alone. Her skill is coveted by their allied clan, and when she comes of age, a marriage of alliance is agreed upon. Her betrothed is a fearsome warrior, the son of one of the greatest Highland chiefs, a man she holds no feelings for but intends to wed all the same.

Highlander warrior shifter Tor Matheson has traveled from the twenty-first century into the past in order to find the one woman who was always meant to be his. He awaits the night of the full moon, the one night when he should be able to sense who she is. Except only one woman draws him irresistibly in, the one woman who is completely and irretrievably forbidden to him. She is betrothed to another and if he wishes to claim her, he'll need to come up against one of the greatest challenges ever thrown at him.

Plunged between two fierce warriors intent on claiming her, Layla must decide whether to allow duty to prevail, or to hand her heart over to the one man prepared to fight for it.

Never has there been such a battle for love.

Books by Joanne Wadsworth

The Matheson Brothers Series
Highlander's Desire, Book One
Highlander's Passion, Book Two
Highlander's Seduction, Book Three
Highlander's Kiss, Book Four
Highlander's Heart, Book Five
Highlander's Sword, Book Six
Highlander's Bride, Book Seven
Highlander's Caress, Book Eight
Highlander's Touch, Book Nine
Highlander's Shifter, Book Ten
Highlander's Claim, Book Eleven
Highlander's Courage, Book Twelve
Highlander's Mermaid, Book Thirteen

Highlander Heat Series
Highlander's Castle, Book One
Highlander's Magic, Book Two
Highlander's Charm, Book Three
Highlander's Guardian, Book Four
Highlander's Faerie, Book Five
Highlander's Champion, Book Six
Highlander's Captive (Short Story)

Billionaire Bodyguards Series
Billionaire Bodyguard Attraction, Book One
Billionaire Bodyguard Boss, Book Two
Billionaire Bodyguard Fling, Book Three

Books by Joanne Wadsworth

Regency Brides Series
The Duke's Bride, Book One
The Earl's Bride, Book Two
The Wartime Bride, Book Three
The Earl's Secret Bride, Book Four
The Prince's Bride, Book Five
Her Pirate Prince, Book Six

Princesses of Myth Series
Protector, Book One
Warrior, Book Two
Hunter (Short Story - Included in Warrior, Book Two)
Enchanter, Book Three
Healer, Book Four
Chaser, Book Five

Highlander's Heart

The Matheson Brothers, Book Five

Joanne Wadsworth

Highlander's Heart
ISBN-13: 978-1-99-003435-0
Copyright © 2015, Joanne Wadsworth
Cover Art by Joanne Wadsworth
First electronic publication: November 2015

Joanne Wadsworth
http://www.joannewadsworth.com

AUTHOR'S NOTE:
This book is a work of fiction. The names, characters, places, and incidents are products of the writer's imagination or have been used fictitiously and are not to be construed as real. Any resemblance to persons, living or dead, actual events, locale or organizations is entirely coincidental. The author does not have any control over and does not assume any responsibility for third-party websites or their content.

Published in the United States of America

First digital publication: November 2015
First print publication: November 2015

Acknowledgements

I have an incredibly supportive family who allow me so much time to write. Huge thanks go to my hubby, Jason, and kiddies, Marisa, Caleb, Cruise and Rocco. Hugs.

For my readers, I can't thank you enough for joining me, and taking this journey to where imagination and magic soar.

Gilleoin – The Legend

In the twelfth century, a man named Gilleoin became the first and only known man to hold bear shifter blood, an ability gifted to him by The Most High One. His clan was called Matheson, and when he mated with a woman carrying faerie blood, they created a line shrouded in secrecy, a line that far into the future, now neared extinction…

Gregor Matheson

The battlefield on the Isle of Skye, Scotland, 1187.

A heavy haze covered the night-shrouded forest on the edge of Loch Eishort where fae-blooded Gregor Matheson stood in his battle attire amongst his clan's allied MacDonald warriors. The horn sounded the alert with one long and eerie blast across the bay, the watchman's second signal the one they'd all been waiting for. Gregor, who held the revered 'power of thought' skill, fisted his great two-handed claymore as the heavy line of MacDonald warriors at his back snarled. He faced them, teeth clenched. "The MacKenzie comes, both your clan's enemy and mine. Douse your torches and maintain a tight guard."

Dunscaith Castle stood tall and strong on a low headland farther along the curve of the bay, the very castle they all defended. Candlelight glimmered from the tower windows of the MacDonald clan's stronghold while the heavy swell of the sea crashed into the cliff-face and sprayed the fortified stone walls.

The Chief of MacDonald stormed along the bay toward their warrior party and halted before Gregor, his fury clearly riding him hard. "I willnae allow the MacKenzie to take Dunscaith. This is MacDonald land and will remain so." The chief clasped Gregor's forearm in a firm warrior hold. "Your fae skill will be needed this night, my friend. Aid where you can."

"You'll always have my aid and that of my clan's. My chief, Gilleoin, sent me to you for a reason, and here is where I'll remain until this battle is done."

"Your ability and all that you can do shall remain safe between me and my men."

"You've kept my secret for many years and I've no doubt you'll continue to do so."

"Aye, I shall. Moving things with your mind alone is an incredible skill, one I greatly admire and respect." MacDonald eyed the white-capped waves rolling into shore, one hand raised to his brow as he tried to search through the eerie mist sweeping in. The thick white fog hazed the air and clogged the brightness of the full moon high above, allowing only the merest trace of light to penetrate through onto the MacDonald's land. "I cannae see the MacKenzie and his men yet."

"Allow me to check." Gregor extended his fae senses out and caught their enemy's approach. "They're very close. We'll be battling hard this night."

"And it'll be a battle we'll win. You take the right wing, Gregor, and I'll take the left. Our enemy will soon learn we'll never allow another to defeat us, or to take what is ours." MacDonald shoved his sword arm high in the air and bellowed, "All to arms. We fight this night, to rid us of our enemy and to hold our land. Let us take these blackguards down."

A thundering roar boomed from the MacDonald's men and reverberated all around.

Gregor swept past the line of fiercely scowling warriors to the right. Out at sea, the MacKenzie's double-mast galley emerged from the mist, the vessel's large square sail a ghostly white and their enemy on board slashing their oars through the tumbling waves. At the helm, a marksman stood with his bow and sent an arrow soaring. It arched high then swished down and thunked into the ground at Gregor's feet. He hauled it from the sand, gripped both ends and snapped it in half over one knee. "Release the arrows," he ordered.

Arrows whizzed over his head, flew high and one after the other, sliced downward and pinged off shields shoved high over their enemy's heads.

The massive war galley caught a cresting wave, skimmed the waters into shore and as the hull scraped the sandy sea floor, a swarm of MacKenzies bounded out and barreled through the knee-deep waves.

"We take Dunscaith!" the MacKenzie chief shouted and surged forward with his men.

A blood-curdling battle cry tore through the stillness of the night, coming from both clans as warriors crashed together in a thundering roar.

Gregor focused his 'power of thought' on the enemy and where each of them battled. With his skill, he could unleash his mind and manipulate whatever he wished, send swords or even men flying. None would ever know what had hit them or whose hand it had been at, yet his fae skill was also a rare gift, one he treasured and used only when his life or one of his nearest and dearest was at stake. Battle he would, but commit outright murder, he wouldn't.

Swords clashed and steel rang loud against steel.

"Be prepared to die!" A MacKenzie warrior swung his sword at Gregor and he heaved forward and met the warrior's attack, their blades crashing together a mere inch from his nose.

"Stand down, or perish." Gregor's arms shook as he shoved one foot back and held his position.

"I will never stand down. I fight, to win this war and to take the MacDonald's stronghold for our clan." His adversary spat at his feet, his gaze venomous. "Your blood and that of every MacDonald here will soon soak this soil."

"That will never happen." With one flick of his hand,

Gregor summoned his skill and whipped his enemy's blade out of his hand then Gregor rammed into the warrior with one shoulder and took him down to the ground. The MacKenzie hit his head on a protruding rock and his eyes rolled to the back of his head. Gregor went down on one knee next to him, checked his breathing. He was alive, but well and truly out of it, and likely to stay that way. One down, so many more to go.

In the deadly dark, warriors fought and blood splattered and swirled within the murky wash of the incoming tide. The war raged and he fought on, not only for their allied MacDonald kin here on the Isle of Skye, but also to keep their enemy from bringing their war to his own Matheson clan's shores across the sea. He'd never allow any harm to come to his kin or the woman he loved. Garia, his wife and soul bound mate, carried their firstborn child and he intended to return to her, just as soon as he could.

Slashing through the enemy's ranks, Gregor bounded closer toward the MacDonald chief.

A fearsome MacKenzie warrior came at the MacDonald and the chief blocked the man's swift blow. Their claymores clashed dead center and another MacKenzie warrior swung in behind the chief. Two against one. 'Twas a calculated attack, one that would weaken their defenses if they lost their chief so soon into the battle. Damn bloodthirsty MacKenzies. They owned such a large parcel of land along the western coastline of the mainland yet still they wanted more, would slay thousands of innocent people to gain the control they so heartily desired.

Gregor flicked one hand out and with his skill sent his allied MacDonald chief flying toward safety. Both the enemy warriors attacking him fell forward into the other, their blades sliding down each other's and piercing their chests. Blood bubbled from the two warriors' mouths as they toppled into a heap. An unfortunate death. One he couldn't have halted with its sheer swiftness.

He raced to the chief's side and together they bounded back into the melee and fought. The battle raged for hour upon hour and Gregor used his skill where he could until the midnight sky lightened and dawn approached.

Bodies littered the shoreline, at least four MacKenzie warriors having fallen to one MacDonald. He'd done his best to aid his allied clan during the skirmish, but he couldn't have been everywhere.

"Retreat!" An ear-piercing whistle suddenly shrilled from one of the MacKenzie's and their enemy all turned tail and raced back toward their galley.

Could it be over? With his sleeve, Gregor wiped blood from his face, his muscles aching and his body weary. Battling, using both his sword arm and his fae skill combined, had worn him out.

A shout went up from the MacDonald warriors as they chased the retreating MacKenzies, and the MacKenzies bounded into their vessel, rowed through the heavy swell and out of the bay.

Shouts of victory filled the air and the men surrounding him gathered their own injured and with them slung over their shoulders, marched back toward Dunscaith Castle and the healers who would be waiting to tend to their casualties.

"I thank you for your aid this day. We've won the battle." The MacDonald chief grasped Gregor's shoulder.

"That we have." Relief filled him, although he didn't doubt this would be one battle amongst many that he'd have to fight against the MacKenzie clan.

"Gregor, I also have a request. I want the power of your fae blood in my line and ask that you consider a betrothal between your firstborn child, the babe your wife now carries, and one of my own children."

"I cannae promise a betrothal, no' when so many of my fae kind are soul bound to another, but should my child no' be mated to another, then aye, I will consider your request." Such a marriage of alliance was one he too heartily desired. 'Twould bind clan MacDonald and clan Matheson together as naught else could.

"Then we shall speak again when the time is right." Lips lifted, the MacDonald sheathed his sword while along the horizon, the sun rose.

A new day had dawned, one they now entered with victory on their side.

Gregor lifted his face high and gave thanks for the new day. Now, 'twas time to return to Garia and his clan. His soul bound wife would need him soon and he intended to be right by her side when she gave birth to their long-awaited child. The first child he hoped would be one of many.

Layla's Birth

In the meadow near the ancient House of Clan Matheson, Scotland, the very night of the battle on the Isle of Skye, 1187.

In the misty, night-shrouded meadow, Garia fell to her knees on the grass as pain gripped her belly and shuddered through her. The cloying mist surrounded her, the air thick and heavy. Mayhap she shouldn't have left the sanctuary of the keep this eve, but she'd awoken with such an ache in her lower back and walking had helped to ease the discomfort.

"Och, child, you cannae be born until after your father has returned to us." Fingertips numb from the icy cold, she rubbed her swollen belly and her babe kicked underneath her palm. "Gregor would no' wish to miss out on your birth. You must wait, wee one."

"Garia!" Nessa, her aunt and their clan's fae-blooded seer, tore through the foggy tree line and hurried across the meadow toward her. "I saw a vision. Your babe wishes to come, willnae wait another moment."

"Nay, my bairn will wait. I've demanded it be so." Tearing pain clawed at her and panting, she fisted the grass, her back arched as the need to push roared to ferocious life within her. "If only my babe would listen."

"I'm so sorry, my dear. I wish I'd seen what ailed you sooner." Nessa knelt before her. "Lie down."

"Your vision. What did you see?" She slumped onto her side and rolled onto her back.

"Your child will be born hearty and hale. I saw her." Nessa flipped the hem of her own gown, tore a strip of cloth from her shift and wiped Garia's sweaty brow. "Your daughter shall hold one of the most coveted of the fae skills, the 'power of thought,' just as her father does. She'll be able to manipulate whatever she wishes, to levitate or move objects if she so desires."

"We have so few in the fae village with that skill." Sheer joy rose within her, right along with another wracking pain. She rocked to alleviate the pressure, only it rose tenfold. "I shall name her Layla, after my mother."

"If your mother and my sister still lived, she would be greatly honored." Nessa swept down her body and knelt between her legs. She lifted Garia's skirts and nodded. "I can see the babe's head. When the next pain comes, I want you to push."

"What else did you see in your vision?" Another pain. Fierce and unrelenting. Breathing hard, she bore down as Nessa had urged her to.

"I saw your daughter as a young lass of mayhap seven or eight. The cherry tree you planted which is just a sapling now at the edge of this meadow shall grow tall and strong, and Layla shall plant a cherry stone from your tree which will take root beside yours. All your hopes and dreams for her, I too shall hold."

"I hold only one hope. That she will be gifted with a soul bound mate, just as I have been gifted with Gregor."

"Aye, I too wish for her to know such a deep and wonderful love. Hold fast and remain strong. Gregor would demand it, and so do I."

"I—" Something gushed from between her legs, hot and

sticky and with the rush of fluid it sapped her strength.

"Nay, there's so much blood." Nessa gasped. "This I didnae see."

Black spots danced before Garia's eyes, her lifeblood pooling underneath her body and coating her fisted hands. "There is little time."

"Stay with me, Garia." Nessa's red locks wisped with gray fluttered about her face. "One more push. Your babe is almost here."

"One more push." For her daughter's sake she would do all she could to bring her safely into this world. She heaved. More pain. So fierce. Her belly tightened and she shoved her elbows into the wet grass, bore down and pushed hard.

A wail rent the air. Hers or her babe's, she wasn't sure.

Stay. She must do as Nessa had bid her.

Only the all-consuming darkness that arose took her swiftly away.

A Prophetic Poem for Layla

The year 1210, twenty-three years later.

A prophetic poem, as written by Nessa, the fae seer, addressed to her goddaughter, Layla, and dispatched by messenger from Nessa's guest chamber at Stirling Castle, Scotland, 1210.

Child of Gregor and Garia.
One day there shall come a warrior,
no' from another land,
but from another place far beyond our time.
He is a fierce steward and shall sail from sea to sea.

Child, you are to remember to whom you are betrothed.
Time is of the essence.
Always look to your heart,
and trust only the man to whom you truly desire.

Where the cherry tree stands, one encounters mystery.
The fates do speak and now is your time.
Dinnae cast aside that which is freely given,
for your happiness is all I seek.

Much love, Nessa.

Chapter 1

Near the ancient House of Clan Matheson, led by Gilleoin, the Chief of Matheson, Scotland, 1210, the day the prophetic poem from Nessa arrives for Layla.

Layla thumped the lush green grass where she lay in the meadow dotted with tiny yellow flowers under the leafy umbrella of the cherry tree her mother had planted so many years ago, the prophetic poem Nessa had written and dispatched to her via messenger from Stirling Castle fisted tight in her hand. If only her godmother was here and not halfway across the Highlands with their chief, Gilleoin, as they visited the king. This poem raised more questions than it did answers.

Her betrothal to Donnan MacDonald, the Chief of MacDonald's son, had been settled upon this past month. Father had wished to ensure she wasn't soul bound to another first and so he'd waited three long years following her coming of age. A soul bond hadn't formed for her amongst her own kind though, a fact she was quietly thankful for. Her parents had been soul bound and following her mother's death after she'd labored with her, Father had mourned Mother to the depths of his soul, would have taken his own life so he might join Mother if it hadn't been for her. He'd chosen that day he'd returned from the battlefield on Skye to raise her with all the love her mother would have, yet had been cruelly denied of. Aye, guilt, in a way, had always gnawed at her over the years, that her birth had brought such heartbreak to Father. She'd witnessed his sorrow throughout her childhood, had no intention of wishing for such a bond when the death of one could bring such pain to the other. Although never could she have asked for such loving parents, that both in their own way had given their lives for hers.

She gripped the thick parchment and traced one finger along the line which haunted her the most.

Dinnae cast aside that which is freely given,
for your happiness is all I seek.

Cast aside what exactly?

She thumped the ground again, breathed deep and forced her mind from the missive back to Mother. During her life, she'd honored her lost parent however and wherever she could, and 'twas in this most sacred place, underneath the cherry tree Mother had planted, that she felt closest to her, wished for that connection, and a moment to silently thank her for all she'd done.

In the canopy high above, the deep red of the ripening cherries bobbed jewel bright against the glossy green leaves and a gentle summer breeze blew. "I miss you, Mother." She sniffed, tears close to the surface, just as they often were when thoughts of her lost parent consumed her as they did this day. "Father misses you too. I wish you were here."

"I miss your mother as well, and wish she were here too." Cherub's voice wisped about her within the breeze then she appeared from the mist and took her full form, her white fur hooded cloak flapping back from her shoulders over top of her regal red gown, her blond hair whipping about her waist. The air settled and the Fae Angel of Love walked toward her with a soft smile, her sparkly skin catching the sunlight and reflecting it back with stunning brilliance. Cherub was an immortal time-walker and the faerie king's daughter. She'd lived over a thousand years and during that time had aided those of her fae-blooded kind who walked this Earth, no matter what century or time that drew her toward. Never had they had such a dedicated guardian to their people as Cherub.

"I cannae believe you're here." She pushed up from the grass and grasped Cherub's hands, her heart a heavy weight in her chest. "I'm sorry if I've called you away from your duties."

"I will always come when you need me. What has you feeling so sad this day?"

"Sometimes there is great pain in having never known someone, of having missed a lifetime of being with them, that I cannae help but be sad. I miss my mother, miss having never known her, miss her touch, seeing her smile, learning at her knee and a thousand other little things I've been denied of. That is what brings me such sadness."

"Aye, yet we must also embrace all that we have been given, including those who love us, and ensure we never let them go. Is it no' better to have loved than to have never loved at all? Your mother, while she walked this Earth, loved you dearly, from the moment she conceived you to the day she brought you into this world. She will love you forever, even though she resides beyond the veil." Cherub pulled her into a hug, her warmth and love encompassing her. "What else worries you? Your need calls to me on the very deepest level, and I sense there is more."

"This morn I received a prophetic poem from Nessa, one she sent by special messenger all the way from Stirling Castle. It has me quite confused."

"Nessa would never have sent you one of her prophecies without good cause. Would you like to share it with me?"

"I've already approached Father about it. He simply nodded and said only time would tell, so aye, I would love some more insight if you have it to offer." She handed the thick piece of folded parchment across.

Cherub unfolded the missive and read, one finger trailing along the words of the first verse. "This speaks of a warrior coming from another place far beyond our time. Nessa must be referring to those unmated warrior shifters from my mate's future clan, although out of Kirk's clansmen from the twenty-first century whom I've brought here, only Tor currently remains unmated." She frowned, her brows pinching together as she eyed her. "Do you feel aught toward Tor? I ask because the very air itself brings to me the secrets it holds, including the call of those who are soul bound. Weeks ago I caught Tor's soul's need for another in this time which is why he is here, although I've yet to be led to exactly whom he's mated to."

"Tor intrigues me, although naught more. I am betrothed to Donnan, have given him my oath that we will wed, and afore the week's end. I have a mere five days afore I speak vows. I certainly cannae forsake my duty to my clan, or the betrothal agreement Father signed."

"Your argument is strong, although I'd like to hear more of this exact 'intrigue' you feel."

"I cannae be Tor's mate, if that is what you're asking."

"I see." Cherub lifted her nose, breathed deep and scented the very air itself, the element she controlled.

"What do you sense?"

"The full moon rises this night and once it does, Tor will finally be able to sense exactly who his chosen one is. No more will she be able to hide from him." Cherub patted her hand then returned her gaze to the missive. "This third verse speaks of this very place, where the cherry tree stands, and that the fates do speak."

"I was drawn here this afternoon, hoped that by coming to

my mother's sacred place that I'd get a little more enlightenment." She leaned back and rested her back against the wide trunk of her mother's cherry tree, its solid presence comforting and surrounding her. "Do you have any more thoughts on the poem?"

"I agree with what Nessa has written. *Dinnae cast aside that which is freely given.*" Smiling, Cherub folded the missive in half and passed it back to her. "And as your father said, only time will tell. That too I wholeheartedly agree with."

"Wonderful." Smiling, she shook her head, tucked the poem into her gown's pocket. "You, Nessa, and Father are so very helpful at times."

"Aye, well, we do try to do our very best when it comes to you."

"Cherub! Layla!" Tor strode through the trees across the far side of the meadow, his hands curved around his mouth and his gaze on the move as he searched for them.

"Over here!" Cherub waved out then rubbed Layla's arm. "I wonder what's brought Tor back so early from the fae village?"

"I've no idea. When he left a couple of days ago, I saw him off and wished him the best of luck. He said he'd remain there until after the full moon rose." The fae village was where he expected to find his chosen one, hoped that he might even be able to sense who she was before the full moon rose, a distinct possibility since two of his kinsmen had recently sensed their mates in such a way. Finlay had known Arabel was his, and from their first meeting. Tavish too, Tor's twin brother, had known Julia was his from the moment they'd met.

"Tor told me the same too." Cherub winked at her, her blue eyes twinkling, and rather mischievously. "Have I ever mentioned that part of mated male's journey in finding his chosen one is in what he must overcome in order to be with her?"

"Aye, a number of times." As Cherub had told their entire

clan.

"Good, because that journey is one that builds the foundation for their bond and all that 'twill be. Hold onto those words. Your happiness too, is all I seek."

"You are turning into Nessa with your prophetic words."

"Well, I thank you for the compliment." Cherub chuckled as she hugged her. "When I see your mother next beyond the veil, I shall tell her you miss her."

"Tell her I love her, with all my heart and soul, and so does Father." She hugged Cherub back. "Thank you for your aid, for coming to me and for looking over the poem."

"Of course, and dinnae forget. *Time is of the essence.*" Cherub dissolved into a mist and streamed around her, kissed her cheek then swept away.

"Where'd Cherub go?" Tor loped toward her under the tree, his billowy white tunic's ties loose at his neck and his black hair sweeping his shoulders. He pressed one hand to the bobbing hilt of his side belted sword and steadied it.

"To the castle, I believe, or wherever Kirk is." Cherub never traveled far from her soul bound mate, and thankfully at the moment Kirk and his brother, Finlay, were in charge of Gilleoin's castle and his lands until their chief returned from Stirling. Which she hoped would be soon. She missed Nessa terribly. Gently, she brushed a scattering of pine needles from Tor's shoulders. "It looks like you've been rolling around on the ground. Have you shifted recently?"

"Aye, my bear is riding me hard, always demanding I make the Change and search for my chosen one. It looks like you've been rolling around on the ground as well." With a grin, he plucked a leaf from her hair and passed it to her.

"I may have." She set the leaf he'd passed her in the center of her palm and touched a finger to one crinkly edge. "Did you have any luck at finding your chosen one at the village?"

"None whatsoever. I didn't sense even an inkling of desire

for one of the lasses who might be the one I'm looking for. I also felt driven to return. I thought I'd speak to Cherub about it, see if she could offer me any advice since she can sense when two are mated. Except she has a terrible habit of disappearing at the wrong time. I'll have to head back to the castle and track her down." He stepped closer, curled his hand over her shoulder, his fingers brushing lightly over her gown and his thumb stroking wider and gliding over the skin of her neck. "But first, I also need to speak to you."

"About?" She lifted the leaf to her lips and blew on it. It fluttered free and with a swish of her fingers and one thought from her mind, she sent the leaf twirling high and whisking away on the gentle afternoon breeze.

Tor watched the leaf flutter high and smiled. "That's an incredible skill you and your father have. The 'power of thought.' I love seeing you move things without any need for touch."

"'Tis a skill we consider a gift, and one we dinnae take advantage of." As it would be so easy to do. She picked up the swaying ends of his tunic's loosened neck ties, the deep V of his neckline exposing a smattering of dark chest hair. "You were saying you wished to speak to me."

"Aye, Gregor mentioned you received a prophetic poem this morning from Nessa. It's the reason why I had to track you down as well." He wrapped his hands around hers as she played with his ties, his palms so warm and big and fully enveloping hers.

"Did Father speak of the details within the poem?" She hadn't asked Father to keep the poem's contents to himself, but she expected he would have all the same.

"He told me only that I should seek you out and take a look at the prophecy Nessa sent you."

"Honestly, I've no desire to share Nessa's prophecy with anyone else yet. I've already shown Cherub and she has offered a little advice. 'Twill do for now." Certainly if the first verse was about him as Cherub believed, then she needed more time to consider all Nessa had shared.

"I promise I'll keep whatever's contained within it between us." He inched closer, until the tips of his black leather boots touched her slippered feet. "Show it to me."

"I know you would, but Nessa has a habit of raising more questions than she does answers with her prophecies. Later. I'll show you another time." She tightened his loose laces, made a bow at the top and as she did he leaned in, touched his nose to her neck and breathed deep. A low rumble vibrated in his chest and she laughed at him. "Are you trying to smell me again, Tor Matheson?"

"My bear loves your scent, has since the first day we met. I'll never forget that moment when you walked into the chief's solar wearing a deep red gown, your golden curls bouncing down your back and a circlet headpiece of pretty red flowers with red and white ribbons fluttering down from the top. You held a tray of ale and oatcakes in your hands, set it down on the chief's desk then walked toward me and proceeded to loosen the ties on my tunic with your mind alone, right before you tightened them in the same way. That was the first time I'd ever come across someone with your fae ability."

She'd never forget their first meeting either. The cook had bid her to take refreshments to Tor and his brother, Tavish, upon their arrival through one of Cherub's portals into their time. All the lasses in the keep had been so curious about the future and the place where these warrior shifters from the twenty-first century had come from. "You sniffed me that day too."

"Your scent is the most tantalizing one I've ever taken in. You smell delicious, like sweet, wild cherries." He lifted his gaze to the canopy high above and the heady scent of the ripening fruit. "Gregor told me about this tree, that his wife planted it here."

"I was also born here."

"Is that why I find you out here so often?"

"Aye, I can sense my mother's presence in this place and that comforts me as naught else can."

"I'm so sorry you lost her the way you did, that she died before either of you ever had the chance to know each other." He motioned toward the second cherry tree, slightly smaller than her mother's but still of a towering height. "Who planted the other tree?"

"When I was seven, my mother's tree bloomed with its first crop and Father picked me a cherry and after I ate it, I planted the stone." She wandered to her tree, reverently touched the rough bark. "A sapling sprouted the following spring and grew strong and tall. This is my tree."

"I'm glad you have this special place to come to, to spend time with your mother and remember her." He caught one trailing end of her white shawl and draped it back over her shoulder.

"At times, when I visit this place, the pain of losing her roars to the surface and becomes stronger. It grips my heart and crushes it, even as it opens my heart wider and revels in my mother's love. I certainly dinnae know how Father has dealt with his loss all these years. They were soul bound and so in love. He would have perished too if it weren't for me."

"The last thing I would want is to lose my soul bound mate, that's once I find her." He brushed his fingers against hers, his thumb stroking fleetingly over the inside of her palm. Tingles radiated out from that tiny spot and sizzled through her, just as they always did when he touched her.

"Tonight is the night you shall find her, your chosen one. You must keep the faith that you will." A part of her heart, deep down inside where she kept her greatest secrets, heaved at the thought of losing him to another, of never having any more of these special moments which they'd had a great deal of together since his arrival. So close, they'd become, and far closer than she should have allowed, only turning away from him had been impossible. Still was. With a soft sigh, she stepped away from him, walked back to her mother's tree and the woven basket she'd brought from the kitchens underneath. She'd promised the cook she'd pick some cherries for a cherry pie, and so she would.

"Tavish said the same thing to me before I came out here in search of you and Cherub, that I needed to keep the faith, that I'd find her. In only a matter of a few hours the sun will descend and the moon rise. Then I will know exactly who she is." Tavish, his twin brother, had recently completed the bond with Julia, one of her closest friends and Nessa's granddaughter. She and Julia had been raised together and she adored seeing how her friend had now found such love with Tavish.

"You should go now, and prepare for the night to come." She grabbed ahold of the cherry tree's lowest limb and with her skill, boosted herself up. From branch to branch, she clambered until she reached the wide bow a good ten feet from the ground and with her deep red skirts bunched around her, plopped into the curved hollow she'd spent many an hour within.

"There's no rush. Do you need a hand?" He nabbed the lowest branch, swung himself agilely up then settled in the bow beside her.

"Nay." She giggled and tapped his nose.

"Oh well, I'm here now." He leaned back, rested his head against the trunk and crossed his wide arms. "I hear you've only got five days left until you wed Donnan MacDonald."

"The MacDonalds are due to arrive from Skye soon. Mayhap on the morrow, or even the day after." Five more days of freedom, five more days of being here amongst her clan, and five more days to bundle a lifetime of memories into with Father and her clan. Wedding Donnan would take her far from Father's side, the one thing about agreeing to the betrothal that she detested with all her heart, not that Skye was too far away. She could return for visits, and she surely would.

"I can see what you're thinking." The wind lifted his silky black hair and tousled it, his gaze filled with concern. "You don't want to go."

"I would dearly love to remain, but my future was set the day my father aided the MacDonald in a battle on the very night of my birth, then cemented further when I came of age and remained alone, without a soul bound mate. Three years Father has waited to see if I shall be bound to another." She tucked a lock of his tousled hair behind his ear. "Glad I am though that I am without such a soul bond. I would hate to go through the heartache and pain my father did when he lost my mother, should I ever lose the one I was bound to."

"There is also heartache and pain in never finding one's soul bound mate. That I know well." A ripe cherry dangled just above his head and he plucked it free, removed the stalk. "All I long for is to find my chosen one, complete the bond and never let her go."

"You dinnae even know her yet. What happens if she is a witch of a woman?"

"She holds the other half of my soul, so witch or not, I can't wait to track her down. She has certainly already bespelled me. Here, take a bite." He nudged the cherry he'd picked against her lips, one of his fingers and his thumb on her chin as he did so. "Open up, Layla. Let me feed you."

"You are one very pushy bear." She gave into him, bit into the cherry then moaned with delight as the sweet juices danced over her tongue.

"Oh goodness, so good. You have to try a cherry too." She searched the closest branches and smiled as she found the largest cherry of the crop. With her mind alone, she tugged the succulent fruit free then brought it bobbing through the air toward her. She settled it on her palm. "There is a tradition surrounding this tree. The stone from the first fruit you eat here must be planted nearby, and since this is your first fruit, you too must do so."

"Does everyone follow this tradition?" He motioned toward her tree. "I only see one other tree."

"Aye, mine is the only stone to sink its roots into the soil and take. Mayhap yours will be the second. You never know." She raised a brow. "Do you wish to take a bite and accept this fruit and the tradition it demands you partake in?"

"Once, when I was a lad, I tossed a plum stone over the curtain wall of Ivanson Castle and it took root. Each summer, that plum tree holds the largest crop of plums I've ever seen, so aye, I'll accept your offering and the tradition." With his golden gaze capturing hers, he opened his mouth, caught her hand and drew the cherry closer. He bit into the fruit, licked a drop of trickling juice from her palm and moaned. "Can you swim, Layla?"

"Pardon?"

"I've a few hours to kill before the sun sets and the moon rises. Join me for a dip after we've picked these cherries." He bit the other half of the cherry still in her hand then greedily eyed the juice seeping between her fingers.

She wanted to snatch her hand back, ensure he didn't touch her in such an intimate way again only she didn't move an inch, had always secretly loved his little touches. Instead, she gave him a warning. "No licking is permitted."

"I love how you taste, just as I love how you smell." He plucked the stone from her hand, slipped it into his pocket. "Higher in the hills, only a short walk from here, I discovered a hidden underground pool behind a waterfall, one filled with steamy, hot water."

"I know the waterfall you speak of but there's no underground pool behind it." She tried desperately hard not to sweep her gaze over him, to take in his magnificently muscled legs encased in black leather, only 'twas a losing battle to do so.

The soft fabric molded itself to every single exquisite inch of him. Oh dear. Betrothed to another man and here she was ogling the one man who was already taken by another. Or at least would be soon.

She sighed. Time to pick the cherries and get on with the job she'd come out here to do.

She flicked her fingers, lifted the woven cane basket from the ground below and sent it gliding underneath the branch holding the heaviest number of fruit. Working her way along the limb, she tugged the cherries free with her skill, one after the other until her basket overflowed.

"That was fast." He rubbed his shoulder against hers, his heady, wild scent surrounding her.

"My skill comes in very handy at times." Gently, she swept the basket back down onto the grass, scrambled over him then with her ability, lifted herself away from the tree and drifted down to the ground.

"Wait up." He swung his legs over the side and in one single bound, jumped and landed with a soft thump beside her. "You haven't said if you'll come with me to the pool I found."

"I'm sorry, but I cannae." She motioned toward the pocket he'd tucked his stone within. "You should plant your stone now afore you leave."

"You choose the spot and I will."

"Plant it close to my tree. The soil there is rich and dark." She walked toward her tree and crouched near it, separated the lush grass and touched one finger to the earth underneath. "This will be the perfect spot."

He dug the stone from his pocket and handed it to her. "While I dig a small hole, you kiss my stone. It's said a fair lass's kiss always brings good luck."

"It does?" She'd never heard that saying afore.

"Aye, my father says so to my mother all the time and he gets kisses aplenty from her." He slid his dirk free of his wrist sheath, knelt next to her and with his arm touching hers, dug a small hole then with a challenging look in his eye, murmured, "Kiss the stone, Layla."

"I hope my kiss brings you all the good luck you wish for." She kissed the stone and held it out to him.

"Perfect." He snuck the stone from her hand, carefully set it in the hole then smoothed the dirt back over the top. "It's also said that a fair lass's ribbon also brings good luck. I'll have the one in your hair, if you don't mind." He extended a hand. "I need all the good luck I can get at the moment, and particularly for the night ahead."

"Of course, but I have a feeling you are making up these sayings just as you please." She unbound the length of red silk loosely woven through her hair and passed it to him. The wind lifted and whipped her golden tresses about her face, the mass of spiral curls bouncing about.

"Maybe, or maybe not, either way you have my thanks." He rose to his feet, tugged her to hers then brought the ribbon to his nose and breathed deep before tucking the ribbon into his pocket. "It smells of you, like fresh air, sunshine, and wild cherries. It's also time for that swim."

"I dinnae have time for a swim. I already told you I cannae come."

"I won't take no for an answer. You're coming whether you like it or not." He scooped her into his arms and strode with her into the trees.

"Tor, wait." She struggled in his arms, but he held her tight and she couldn't get down. "Set me back on my feet. I have much to do this day and swimming with you isnae one of those things."

"I'm not setting you back down. You also might want to grab your basket of cherries before you lose sight of them." With a determined step, he marched along the pine-needle covered trail, the canopy a thick leafy green high above.

"Are you always this unreasonable?" She hooked her arms around his neck and struck a look over his shoulder so she could catch the basket up with her skill. With one thought from her mind, she lifted it and sent it swishing through the air and bobbing along beside them. She huffed then nipped his ear. Actually nipped him. She'd never done such a thing to a man before.

He growled, deep in his chest, and fur rippled across his arms, there one moment and gone the next. His golden shifter eyes blazed and his lips lifted in a challenging smile. "I see you wish to tangle with a bear."

"And I see you wish to tangle with one who holds the 'power of thought.' I can tell you now who'll win the battle."

* * * *

"Me." Tor had no intention of losing any battle with her. From the day he'd arrived through one of Cherub's portals into this time, Layla had intrigued him. He'd been awed by both her and her ability, his bear always rolling around under his skin whenever she was close and for the past three days while he'd been at the fae village farther along the loch, searching amongst the lasses for his chosen one, something within him had niggled at the distance he'd instilled between himself and the very woman in his arms. That niggle had grown in strength the moment he'd returned and heard from her father that a missive from Nessa had arrived for her. A prophecy, Gregor had told him, and one he'd find of the utmost interest. Holding the woman in his arms closer against his chest, his bear once again surging to the surface, he sensed only a deep need to never let her go. "Are you hiding something from me, Layla? Because if you are, I'm going to find out exactly what it is before this night is done."

"And what would I possibly have to hide from you?" She crossed her arms with a slap, all while directing the basket of cherries that bobbed along beside them through the air. "Donnan will also be furious to learn I've allowed another man to cart me about like this. I am nearly a married woman, which means your behavior right now is totally unacceptable and inappropriate."

"When I first learnt you were betrothed to Donnan MacDonald, a huge level of frustration flushed through me."

"Well, I've no idea why that would be." One serious glare came at him.

"Perhaps I should have paid more attention to that frustration than I did, because right now you seem to be the only woman here who I'm continually drawn to. You and only you." He plowed on along the scrub-lined trail leading deeper into the woods, the pathway meandering upward into the hills high behind the castle. Overhead, birds twittered in their nests and the canopy thickened, blocking almost any and all trace of the late afternoon sun above. "What I feel for you, it's growing stronger each and every day, Layla. I can't seem to stay away from you even though I'm supposed to be at the village where my mate most likely resides."

"You said you cannae sense her there, and I realize your mate is hiding from you, somehow and some way, but that does no' mean that she is me."

"You sound so certain, yet right now I'm wondering if you might just be the very one I've been seeking. Perhaps your betrothal to another is how you've been hiding from me. Certainly whatever this is between us, I'm going to delve deeper into it and find out exactly what's going on."

"This is naught, and one cannae hide behind a betrothal. I have also given Donnan my oath to wed him afore the week's end, of which I shall." She jabbed a finger into his chest. "Would you at least allow me to walk while we have this argument? Reason is all you need to see, and I'll make sure you do."

"If I put you down, I want your promise that you'll continue on with me to the waterfall."

"I promise." She snorted under her breath. "You are a very

vexing man."

"Thank you."

"It wasnae a compliment."

Grinning, he set her feet on the ground, her long blond spiral curls sliding sensuously over his forearms as he did. He adored her fiery nature, her temper which rose quickly to the surface then just as quickly died away. She was like a fierce sunrise and a thundering storm, all beauty and explosion rolled into one, then the ultimate grace as she simmered back down. She was the kind of woman he longed for, with attributes he hoped his chosen one held. The kind of woman he would love to roll around in a meadow with, to claim as his and make her his wife. The kind of woman he could make love to each and every day and still never get enough of. Those thoughts barreled through his mind, gaining with strength and making him want her all the more. Hell, if she wasn't his mate, it would likely kill him.

With one hand at the small of her back, he guided her along the winding trail leading upward toward the craggy hilltop. As she walked beside him, the skirts of her red velvet gown swished against his legs and her cinched bodice lifted her breasts, the white satin trim along the low-cut neckline brushing the upper swells of her creamy skin.

His mouth watered at the heavenly sight. He might have let her down, but he didn't think he'd ever be able to let her go, not until they'd talked and he'd discovered exactly what it was about her that had both him and his bear clamoring for more of her. She had to be the one, his mate, and the holder of the other half of his soul.

"Cease looking at me like that, Tor." She frowned, and so beautifully.

"How exactly am I looking at you?"

"Like you want to eat me."

"I believe I do."

"And cease speaking in such a way as well." She gripped her skirts and stomped ahead. "I've witnessed Cherub and Kirk's mated bond taking form, Tavish and Julia's too, not to mention the others whom Cherub has brought through from your time. Their love for each other is so precious to behold. We do no' have such a bond."

"The mated bond is what my shifter clan live for." He lifted his nose to the air and drew in the dampness of the forest floor, the clear aroma of pine and the fresh scent of the air, although Layla's intoxicating cherry scent swirled around and stamped its wild beauty over it all. "I should have remained here these past three days rather than left you all alone. I'll never leave you again."

"No more." She huffed, continued on. "I am no' your mate."

"What if you are? You need to at least consider the possibility."

"I need to consider naught." Another huff and a vexing stare.

Damn, she had the most beautiful eyes, the dark brown so rich in color and swirling with a multitude of emotions. Well, it seemed he had a very feisty woman on his hands, and possibly a mate, of which he'd know with absolute certainty the moment the full moon rose. Tonight was the one night of the month when his chosen one would never be able to hide from him. He'd sense the exact direction he needed to take in order to track her down, although all his senses roared that he was already in full pursuit, the woman before him the very one who held the other half of his soul. Hell, whenever he was around her, all he wanted to do was touch her in some way, keep her close, learn all he could about her. She intrigued him as no other could.

"Layla, wait a moment. Let me clear the way so you don't catch your skirts on the scrub." Thick brush partially clogged the last portion of the pathway and he swung his sword free and slashed the scrub away then gestured for her to go first.

"Oh my." She stepped through and gasped. "'Tis so stunning."

She was the stunning one. He joined her where the forest fell away and the roaring waterfall pummeled down. Water rushed over the topmost edge of the waterfall a good ten to fifteen feet above their heads. It sleeted past a stone ledge hidden underneath the fall of it and crashed into a pool thirty feet below, before streaming around thick boulders and flowing downhill toward the inner channel of Loch Alsh.

"'Tis been such an age since I last tramped up here. I'd clear forgotten how incredibly beautiful this place is."

"I'm glad you agreed to come with me."

"Agreed?" Hands on her hips, she arched a brow at him. "So, now we are here Mr. Come-swimming-with-me, tell me exactly where this hidden pool is."

"It's best I show you rather than tell you. Nice new title you've given me there, Miss I-want-to-eat-you." He tapped her nose, nabbed the basket of cherries from the air which she still had bobbing beside them and set it safely on the ground next to the partially hidden ledge. "Are you willing to follow where I lead?"

"I have thus far, and you arena *eating me*, no' even a bite. Make sure your bear understands that as well."

"All he understands is that you nipped my ear first. That I consider a bite." He caught her up in his arms, his hold around her firm and leapt onto the ledge. Swiftly, he set her down on her feet, pressed her back against the slick rock wall behind her and ensured they both remained steady on their feet. "I thought it best to just jump rather than warn you. Are you all right?"

"Of course, and this place is truly a haven of beauty." She grinned at him then swayed forward and glanced at the sheer drop downward. The crashing spray drifted upward and coated her skin, wetting the luscious swell of her breasts and the long column of her neck.

His mouth watered for a taste of her, to lick her flesh and nibble away. Instead, he motioned toward the cherries. "Bring your delicious haul here."

"One moment." She lifted one hand and with her skill sent the basket up and sailing across to them.

"I'll take them." He swung the basket out of midair, caught her hand with his free one and shuffled sideways under the cascading fall of water toward the slim and almost unnoticeable entrance to a tunnel he'd found at the end. "Take care with your step, my sweet."

"I shall, and I am no' your sweet."

"We're almost there." Between two cracks in the rock wall slick with the water's spray, he squeezed through and tugged his sweet yet feisty woman in after him.

"Never would I have known this was here." She scampered around to his other side and stared down the darkened passageway carved of black stone. "I wonder if any of my clansmen have found this tunnel afore. Certainly none have ever spoken of it if they have."

"There's no sign of any disturbance deeper within. Come. You need to see the pool I found." He led the way down the tunnel and at the end, jumped onto the grainy white sand a good six feet below.

Overhead, the craggy ceiling of the cavern rose to a high peak with a three-foot wide hole at the top where a wispy trail of steam from the hot water vented out. It had been that trace of steam he'd first noticed from outside that had sent him on a mission to find its source. As the steam disappeared on the breeze, what remained of the late afternoon sunshine streamed in and glimmered across the glassy surface of the pool and the slick rock walls surrounding them.

"This is such an enchanting place."

The woman before him was far more enchanting. Aye, he

could barely take his gaze from her, and bringing her here to this sacred place filled him with such a sense of rightness. No one else did he wish to be with right now, other than her. He set the basket on the golden-white sand beside the wall, returned to her and held out his hands. "Jump, Layla. I'll catch you."

"Nay, I can manage the distance on my own. Never forget my skill, Tor." She brushed a stringy cobweb aside and leapt from the edge and gently glided down and landed with a soft swish on the sand before him.

Slippers kicked off and her shawl tossed near the wall, she twirled around, her arms outstretched and her deep red skirts flaring, her abundance of glorious spiral tresses whispering through the air, a wavy, golden ripple that completely enticed him, just as the rest of her did, both inside and out. He caught her around the waist, ran his hands over the velvet of her gown and caressed her hips, although not for long. She snuck out of his hold, dashed toward the gently lapping water and skirts bunched in her hands, tickled her toes in it. "'Tis terrible that this is the first time I've ever been here."

"This cavern is well protected from both sight and the elements." He removed his sword belt, propped it against the rock wall and divested himself of his wrist dagger and boots. His need to touch her again raged through him. Hell, the signs that he'd finally found his chosen one were adding up, one after the other, and in an insurmountable mountain. "Are you coming in for a swim?"

"I have naught to swim in, other than my shift underneath." She walked out of the water and stopped in front of him.

"You keep your shift on and I'll keep my pants on." He pulled his shirt from his leather pants, hauled the white linen over his head and tossed it on top of his weapons.

"Do you swim with the lasses often?" She swayed closer, her gaze on his chest and her warm breath fluttering over his skin.

"You shall be the first, unless you count my mother and the odd cousin." He picked up the laces at the front of her bodice and tugged the bow free, all while wishing he could tug all her clothes from her, to be able to touch her skin without any barrier, to rub his body against hers. Damn, he had it bad. "Where's your favorite swimming spot?"

"I dinnae have a favorite, although following this swim, it might very well be here." She took the loosened ties from him, shrugged her arms out of the long draping sleeves and wriggled the velvet down and past her hips until it fell into a pool of shimmery red at her feet.

He crouched, picked it up after she stepped clear of it, folded the velvet and set it next to the rest of their belongings against the wall.

"Thank you." She waded into the water, went deeper, until her shift swished about her legs then she dove and disappeared underneath the surface. Water rippled across the glassy top as she swam through the darker depths below.

His chest tightened and his fingers itched. He didn't care to have her moving so far from him, wanted only to grab ahold of her and return her to his side. He prowled the sandy edge of the pool, welcoming the fierce emotions that arose. Aye, Layla was his mate, his bear too demanding it was so. She was the one he'd been searching for all this time and eluding him as well. He wouldn't allow her to elude him any longer.

In a spray of water, she shot to the surface, waved out to him. "Are you coming in?"

"I'll be right there." He had to try and curtail some of this desperate need for her, otherwise he'd frighten her with how strong his desire for her pulsed within him. He bounded in, dove and kicked under the water and emerged before her, grasped her around the waist and treaded water for the both of them. "I want no secrets between us. Do you understand that?"

"I'm not keeping any secrets from you, that I'm aware of."

"Then tell me how you feel right now."

"Wet." An impish smile lifted her lips.

"Do you love Donnan?" He gave her hips a squeeze, hoped like hell she harbored not one single feeling for the man.

"Donnan and I have spent time together whenever he's visited, and he seems considerate, but I'm also well aware he's a hardened warrior, blood-thirsty and very determined. He wouldnae be the son of a great chief otherwise. The chiefs of clan MacDonald hold the title of Lords of the Isles, and they do so for a reason. **They are a force to be reckoned with, which includes Donnan.**"

"What happens if I asked you not to see him again?"

"I would say you had no right to request such a thing."

"I also wish to ask for a kiss."

"Nay, Tor. We arena mated and you must cease thinking so." She pushed him away, dove under the water and kicked toward the overhanging ledge at the side of the pool. She emerged, clambered up onto the slick black rock, water sluicing to her feet as they dangled in the water.

"Let me make one thing absolutely clear, Layla." He couldn't allow her to harbor any other notion than that which was the truth. "We are mated and there is nothing you can say which will change that fact."

Through the vent high above, the sun dipped below the horizon and a heavenly glow of golden-red speared through the darkening sky. The moon rose and shimmered, the stars, one by one, glowing and twinkling all around it.

His claws sliced out from his fingers, his bear fairly demanding his release. He'd never shifted in front of her before, always done so in the depths of the forest when he was well and truly alone, but no more. Gently, he gripped her wet knees through her shift. "I need to make the Change and it can't wait any longer. My bear wishes to meet you."

"You intend to shift now?"

"Aye, and since I detest shredding my clothes, the pants have to go. Close your eyes if you need to."

"This is completely inappropriate."

"If we weren't mated, I'd agree."

"How many times must I tell you we arena soul bound?"

"You can tell me as often as you'd like, but deep inside my heart I know the truth, and very soon, so will you."

She huffed again, shoved her wet hair from her face and glared at him. "You are completely impossible."

"Aye, but now I'm your impossible. Are you ready?"

"If you truly must shift then do so, just make sure your bear does no' bite me."

"My bear could never hurt you, but I will be biting you at some point in time, and likely the first opportunity you allow it." He backed up a step, unlaced the ties at his waist and shoved his pants off under the water then lobbed them through the air toward his discarded clothes on the sand. The leather hit the beach with a wet thump and he turned back to the only woman he would ever desire, the one and only woman who held the other half of his soul.

It was time. For both of them to accept their destiny, one he couldn't wait to embrace. She was his mate and now no longer could she hide from him. He'd found her, and he wasn't letting her go, not to Donnan MacDonald or any other man.

* * * *

Layla should never have allowed Tor to take her from the meadow. Now, she was trapped here in this remote cavern with a determined man and his resolute bear so very close to the surface. She couldn't be his mate, no matter his desire for her was clear to see and apparently continuing to deepen. "Wait right there, Tor."

She needed to keep some space between them.

"My bear will want your touch."

"I mean it." She did, only as the moon blazed brighter, a

heavy orb of golden-yellow, her very soul ached at the thought of keeping him at bay.

"There will be no marriage between you and Donnan MacDonald." Tor surged forward, grasped her dangling legs. "This is our night, and the sooner you acknowledge it, the better." Challenge lit his gaze and his luscious lips lifted, not that she should have noticed his lips. Except she always had, wished only to lean forward and lick them.

"What are you doing to me?" He had her thoughts in total disarray.

"It's our bond taking form, your soul calling to mine and mine to yours." He rubbed upward, over her knees, his thumbs swirling in a slow circle along the inside of each leg and his golden eyes heating to a smoldering hue. "When one shifts, it causes quite a lightning bright display. Close your eyes or turn away if you need to, but be warned, my other half might get a little possessive over you. He knows you're ours and that you're fighting to keep your distance from us. He's also far more insistent and forceful than I am."

"I can handle your bear. I'm rather insistent and forceful myself. Shift. Show me your other half."

"Of course, and by the way"—he winked at her—"demanding I show you my other half is a very mate thing to demand." He stepped back and shifted, bright lights bursting a myriad of sparks before one very large bear with silky black fur reared up onto its hind legs in the water and roared. He came back down, his paws slapping against the stone ledge either side of her, his teeth sharp and snapping together.

"Calm down." She wriggled back, her back coming up hard against the slick stone wall and her heartbeat racing. Nowhere else could she move to get away from him.

His bear whined as if he'd not meant to scare her then he slowly closed his eyes, nudged her belly with his muzzle and plopped his head into her lap, made a soft whimpering sound that touched her very heart and pulled it closer toward him.

"Well, that is much better. Thank you." She couldn't help but lay her hands on his head, pat between his ears, his fur, so silky soft to the touch, tickling her fingers. Gently, she stroked down his neck and under his chin, and a sensuously hungry purr rumbled from deep within his chest. The sound caused a wicked heat to surge through her, not one she wished for but one that came all the same. 'Twas also the kind of heat she'd never experienced before. It settled between her inner thighs and made her gasp.

Tor sniffed and rumbled deeper.

"Ignore that," she whispered.

He licked her wet shift bunched in her lap then rubbed his cheek across her belly.

"I mean it. Ignore that." She tried to push his head away but only sank her hands deeper into his silky pelt. Touching him so freely felt so good, like she'd been given a gift she never wished to relinquish.

Rising higher, he sniffed up her torso and around her breasts before sticking his wet nose against her neck. His tongue lolled out, swiped across her chin and ear, then face to face, his golden eyes blazed in the moonlight.

"I wish you could talk to me, tell me what you're thinking." She patted down his back and along his sides. The need to keep stroking him comforted her and quite clearly him as well since he arched into her touch and wished only for more of it. Digging her nails in deeper, she gave him the more he seemed to want, scratched harder and when she did, one long rumble vibrated from deep within his chest, his pleasure in her touch clear to see.

Eyes closed, he flopped his head down into her lap again and her need to ensure he always remained so content rose to a fierce level within her. She bent and cuddled into him. There was naught more stunning to see than his bear and as the full moon blazed overhead, her heart and soul lifted. She craved more of this, only—oh dear, what was she thinking? She'd already given her word to wed another man. How could she turn around and go against that vow? And what of her clan if she did?

"We are in a terrible predicament, Tor." A softly murmured decree in his ear. "How do we move forward from this moment when duty demands I honor my betrothal agreement with Donnan?"

He growled and bright lights blazed as he made the Change then looming over her, his damp locks falling forward rakishly over his brow, he eyed her. "We move forward with care and consideration, never forgetting that it is the two of us who are soul bound. There can be only one, for both of us."

"That is easy for you to say but an entirely different situation to deal with. The betrothal agreement between Donnan and I is almost as binding as the marriage vows themselves are. There is a signed contract."

"I wish to have an agreement between us that takes precedence over that one, with a vow I will give to you right now." He caught one of her hands, lifted it to his cheek and rubbed against her palm, his gaze filled with need and desire. "Layla, from this day forth, whatever path you tread will be the same that I do. You have my full protection, that of my body, my clan, my family, and all that I am. I give myself to you freely. You're my mate and no other's. I ask that you accept me, for I will always be here, fighting for you."

"You're all I could ever desire in a mate, but..." Tears misted her gaze and trickled free. "I'm not free to speak any vow to you in return."

"Don't cry." He shook his head, pain and sorrow flaring across his face. "Please, whatever you do, don't cry."

"You're a warrior, and warriors live such short lives when they willingly lay down their life for their clan. One day you will go off to war and I'll be left to await your return, or to await the return of your body should you perish in a battle."

"I will always return home to you. That is something you should never fear." He scooped her off the boulder and heaved around the edge of the pool through the water toward the beach.

"You cannae make that kind of promise when—wait. You arena wearing a stitch of clothing." She shoved her eyes closed as he carried her out of the pool and set her on her feet on the sand. She swayed as he left her, patted the air as she tried to find him. "Are you dressing?"

"I don't wish to, but aye, I am." A rustle sounded then he caught her around the waist and touched his lips to her ear. "I have my shirt on and it reaches me mid-thigh. Open your eyes, but just know if you do, I will kiss you."

"Pardon?"

"You heard me." Whisper soft words that made her blood heat with a heady rush. "If you open your eyes, Layla, then I'll kiss you. I need this, to feel your lips on mine." His arms tightened around her back as he tipped her farther backward and off her feet, his warm mouth trailing along her cheek to the corner of her lips.

"I have no' opened my eyes."

"I know, but the question is, do you want to? Or better yet, will you?" He licked along her lower lip and she gasped at the sweetly sensual touch. More heat and her body argued fervently against what was in her head. She wanted to wrap herself around him and never let go.

"If I give you an inch, you'll clearly take a mile. That is easy to see."

"Aye, it appears you already know me quite well." He sucked her lower lip into his mouth and she cried out at the exquisiteness of it.

"Give me mercy," she whispered raggedly and dug her hands into his hair. She held on as if her very life depended on it. "Please, you must halt and release me."

"Open your eyes." His breath fluttered warmly over her wet

lower lip. "I want you to see me, who I am, and how much I desire you."

Chapter 2

Layla already knew who Tor was and how much he desired her, but as yet, she couldn't return his affections, not when she'd promised herself to another. She opened her eyes, snuck her hands between them, allowed her 'power of thought' to rise and pushed him back with her skill before he could claim a kiss then ducked out of his arms and backed up. "Two can play at your game, Tor Matheson."

"Escaping me now will be impossible." Prowling in a circle around her, he snorted under his breath. "I wouldn't even try it if I were you."

"I never said I wanted to escape you, just for you to give me some mercy. Some time too would be rather helpful. I need to consider all that has happened and what I must now do going forward." She turned around as she followed his very predatory move, each of his circles drawing inward and bringing him closer to her. Her mate was well over six feet in height, all sleek, hard muscle, his white tunic gaping at the V neckline and his hem dangling mid-thigh and displaying his long, muscled legs. His wide shoulders and gorgeous shifter eyes half-lowered in an incredibly sensual way, took her breath away. He was beautiful, his bristles shadowing his firm jaw with black stubble and his lips well-defined. She wanted to kiss him, just as much as she *didn't* want to kiss him. Drat these conflicting emotions.

"Tell me what's going on in your mind." He continued to circle her.

"While I'm betrothed to another, naught can happen between us. I willnae be disloyal to the man I've agreed to wed."

"I applaud your loyalty, only you're giving it to the wrong man. Yours is a betrothal that needs to end, my challenging mate, and soon. I certainly won't walk away from you simply because you're not willing to take a risk and accept the mated bond."

"This has all happened so suddenly, and I have Donnan to consider, as well as you, and my entire clan."

"You will decline the betrothal agreement with Donnan MacDonald, because I'll never sit idly by knowing you're about to wed another man."

"I'm supposed to speak vows with Donnan afore the week's end." Stupid full moon. How she wished she could go back into hiding from him so she needn't be forced to bring such dishonor to her clan by breaking her oath. "You're asking me to choose you and forsake my duty."

"What of your duty to me?" Hands on his hips, he halted and eyed her.

"I didnae have a duty to you until that silly moon rose this night." Huffing, she brushed past him and paced the beach.

"That I can agree with, but now you do." He caught her hand as she made her next pass and brought her fingers to his lips, nibbled on the tips.

"It willnae be easy for me to break the betrothal, Tor."

"I'll make it easier by speaking to Donnan on your behalf." He leaned in, his nose a mere inch from hers and his wet hair curling damply around his shoulders. "Don't cast me aside."

Cast aside?

Dinnae cast aside that which is freely given, for your

happiness is all I seek.

Nessa's words reverberated through her mind and she gasped, clutched a hand to her mouth.

"What is it?" Tor demanded.

"'Tis a firm answer to a question from my godmother's prophecy." The bond was freely given and Nessa had told her not to cast it aside. So too she'd said, *Always look to your heart, and trust only the man to whom you truly desire.*

Who did she truly desire? Donnan was a man who could never steal her heart, nor bring her a lifetime of pain should she ever lose him in a battle. Losing Tor would cripple her. He held the other half of her soul, just as she now held the other half of his. Desire him, she already did, had for some weeks, not that she'd allowed herself to acknowledge it until this moment. She'd pushed those feelings deep down, told herself she found him intriguing and naught else. What a lie. Every time he'd been near, it had been impossible not to touch him in some way, and so too he'd been as free with his affections as she had been with hers. Little touches here and there. Whispered conversations during the evening meal in the great hall. Walks in the forest or along the shoreline once the sun had set and the moon had risen. She'd missed him these past three days, wished only for him to return from the village. In a way, it had hurt that he'd even left. Stupid, dratted bond. 'Twas an impossible thing, only she'd been overlooking what was right before her eyes and now she no longer could.

Shoulders slumped, she gave into the truth, squeezed her eyes shut and bowed her head. "I'm sorry, Tor. I've been ignoring what was right before my eyes and shouldnae have."

"You're not the only one. So have I." He leaned in, touched his forehead to hers. "I've been driven toward you time and time again since my arrival but because of your betrothal, I've kept myself from accepting what was right before my eyes. Now I no longer can. The full moon doesn't lie, and neither does the truth I see so glaringly well now. You are my chosen one. Allow me to court you, Layla, to show you the truth within my heart. There is no woman I would rather have at my side than you. I'd also like to ask that you spend this night with me, right here in this cavern, just the two of us. We need the time together. Only us."

Could she? Should she? The answer came to her lips before she could hold it back. "Aye, but no kissing."

"You strike a hard bargain, but I agree, although if you change your mind on that count, then tell me. Immediately." He stepped away from her, collected his pants, flapped the sand from the leather, shoved his long muscled legs into each pant leg and fastened the ties at his waist.

"Are you going somewhere?" He couldn't leave now, not after all they'd discovered.

"Only to hunt our evening meal. I promise I won't be long." He swept up his sword belt, nabbed a cherry from the basket which he pocketed and strode past her barefoot. As he reached the entrance to the tunnel, with her mind alone she rolled one of the larger rocks from near it underneath the high lip and he bounded onto the rock, jumped into the passageway and over his shoulder, smiled at her. "Thank you, and stay here. Don't move an inch."

"I'll be waiting." She rested back against the rock wall at her back and softly sighed.

Time is of the essence.

Aye, in five days' time she was due to speak vows with Donnan before a clergyman, vows her heart revolted at now having to utter. Her soul bound mate had finally come for her, and now she only hoped he hadn't arrived too late.

* * * *

Tor strode down the tunnel, the pounding fall of the waterfall ahead echoing toward him. He'd been given so little time to woo his mate. Certainly losing her to another man wasn't an option. He'd never be able to let her go, would steal her away before Donnan MacDonald ever could.

Taking a deep breath, he stepped out of the tunnel and into the clear night air, the waterfall a rippling sheet of water that arched from over his head and down into the steep ravine below. He walked to the end of the ledge and leapt onto the scrub-lined trail. Overhead, the night sky glittered with an array of stars, the full moon a bright and beautiful orb of gold rising higher with each minute that passed. The full moon had always offered his shifter kind the promise of finding their chosen one, a journey they all undertook under its heavenly glow when the time to find their mate had arisen.

Tonight, he'd be with the one woman who was always meant to be his, or at least he would as soon as he'd caught them some dinner. He set out along the trail, rummaged and found a ropy tree root hanging loose along the side of the cliff then chose the perfect sapling when he came across it, one that would whip up nice and fast when attached to a noose snare. He fashioned the noose from the ropy tree root then with twigs hammered into the ground, draped the noose over the trap. A toss of dry leaves to hide the trap, the cherry he'd pocketed on his way out in place on the top as bait, and he was done.

While he waited for the trap to catch their meal, he trod down the trail, reached the ravine at the bottom of the waterfall and swung his skin free of his belt, dipped the pouch in the stream and filled it up. Layla had asked for some time and he'd give it to her but while he did, he'd court her, exactly as she deserved and exactly as his heart and soul demanded he do. Showing her exactly who he was and how much he desired her would drive him over the days ahead. Five days in total. That's all he had.

Needing to ensure she was all right and not still fretting over the discovery of their soul bond, he headed back along the trail, collected twigs and the odd log along the way and returned to her.

He bounded into the cavern, found her dipping and diving and exploring the cavern's pool just as he'd done the first time he'd found this sacred place. He waved out and she swam toward him, emerged from the water, her golden tresses slick down her back and her beautiful brown gaze moving over him. "Are you enjoying your swim, Layla?"

"Very. How's your hunt faring?"

"The trap is set. I'll light a fire with this wood I've brought." Arms full, he knelt at the rear of the cavern and tucked the wood into a pile beside him. He dug a small pit in the sand and set to work building the fire as she plopped down next to him. He pulled the stringy bark off a log, struck flint with his dirk and coaxed the sparks into life. After building the fire into a crackling blaze with the twigs and wood, he held out his pouch to her. "Would you like some fresh water?"

"Very much." She popped the plug and brought the mouthpiece to her lips. How he wanted to bring her lips to his, to kiss her and—damn it. He needed to leave before he toppled her onto her back and took her right here and now.

"I'll be back soon." He jogged out of the cavern, back into the crisp night air, the rush of the waterfall and the peace and solitude of this sacred place settling over him and calming his fierce need at least a little. Being able to touch their chosen ones was vitality important to his shifter kind. Would be a difficult need to tamp down while she insisted he must.

A soft snap dinged from the direction of his snare and he let out a heartfelt sigh. Thank heavens. Dinner was caught. While he tended to that, he'd be able to honor his word and keep his hands and lips off her.

He tramped down the trail, removed the rabbit, took it down to the ravine's stream and skinned and cleaned it. Done, he returned to the cavern and found his woman sitting cross-legged before the fire, her shift now drying and fluffed around her, her hands raised to the flames and a sweetly intriguing look on her face. "Are you warm enough?" he asked her.

"Aye, I'm quite warm." Smoke wafted from the fire and swirled with the steam rising from the pool. "I have questions, Tor, about you and your time. Do you mind if I ask you one or two of them?"

"Ask however many you like." He chose some of the sturdy sticks he'd brought in earlier and created a spit for the rabbit.

"How careful are you when you fight for your clan?"

"We fight in a slightly different way as to how wars are fought in this time." He threaded the rabbit into place and set it to cook over the fire then eased in beside her, his legs extended and crossed at the ankle as he rested his back against the wall. "We join together in teams in order to work high-level government cases. Those cases ensure our country's villains and criminals get locked away." He removed his sword-belt, propped it against the wall within arm's reach then unsheathed his dirk and whittled away at a small chunk of wood. That'd help him keep his hands busy for certain, and off her.

"Then would you say you're a...*fierce steward* for your clan and country, a keeper and a guardian?" The firelight flickered over her creamy skin, lit her drying hair with a golden halo.

"Aye, a fierce steward is a good term. At times I oversee these high-level teams as we work together to ensure our mission's success, missions that sometimes lead us farther afield than Scotland."

"You mean to say you, ah, *sail from sea to sea*? To other places?"

"Aye, that is exactly what I'm saying." Two slightly strange questions, or at least the way she'd worded them they had been. *Fierce steward. Sail from sea to sea.* Was there possibility another meaning behind her questions?

"Will your team be missing you right now?"

"Whenever one of our clan is away from Ivanson Castle,

they are missed. Is it not the same here for you? I'm sure should you be away for some reason then your kin would miss you." He carved the piece he whittled into the rough shape of a bear then worked on shaving it into even more intricate detail. The muzzle took form, the ears alert and standing up, just as his bear's did.

"Aye, my father already grieves for my leaving, but the Isle of Skye is where Donnan lives and thankfully 'tis no' too far away." She dipped her head, plucked at her shift's skirts. "At least Father can visit me on Skye, whereas should I accept our bond, I would be over eight-hundred years distant from him."

"I'd never allow your father to lose you, and Cherub gladly transports Tavish and Julia back and forth, Finlay and Arabel too. I have no doubt Cherub would do the same for you."

"You're right. Cherub is devoted to her kin, no matter where they live." She lifted her gaze to his, tears suddenly welling within.

"What's wrong?" Hell, if he'd upset her again by one of his comments then he'd need to take his own blade to himself. "Your protection, your needs, and your heart's desire will always come first with me. You are the missing part of me that I've been searching for. I need you to know that."

"I do, Tor." She reached out a hand, his name rolling off her tongue so softly, so sensuously as she touched his arm. Never had another spoken his name with such an underlying current of need before.

"What else worries you?" He gripped her fingers, squeezed, her hand so very tiny in his.

"I have so much to think about. That is all." She frowned, pulled her fingers from his and turned the roasting meat over.

He returned to his carving, shaved down the bear's legs, accentuating the silky pelt and adding paws and claws as he considered how he was supposed to continue comforting her while remaining completely honest.

"Have any of your kinsmen ever discovered their mate was

already taken?" She nibbled on her lower lip. "As I am."

"You're not taken yet, and there is only one for us, the other our soul cries out for."

"None of your clan have ever accepted another, other than their soul bound mate?"

"We accept only our chosen one in order to keep our bloodline's ability to shift in place. That is why our shifter line now nears extinction. It has come to the point that if we're now to survive, we need a new infusion of fae blood in our line to strengthen it. Our last clan birth occurred over five years ago, and that can't be allowed to continue."

"You wish for children?"

"Absolutely. I adore children, love their energy and exuberance." He couldn't wait to have a child he could guide in this world, one he could love and adore right alongside his woman. "What of you?"

"Children bring such joy to one and all, and my father longs for grandchildren. He has told me so many a time." She wriggled closer. "In all honesty, I also agreed to the betrothal with Donnan so I might be given the chance to have children of my own. My mother loved me, gave her life for mine, and I wish to honor her love by sharing my own love with my children."

"Then I promise to give you as many children as you wish for, or cubs since our offspring will be as I am and hold the heart of a shifter." He held out the finished wooden bear for her, one he'd carved meticulously for her alone. "This is for you, to remind you of me. Will you accept my gift?"

"'Tis a beautiful carving." She leaned forward, her drying hair sweeping over his forearm as she plucked the bear from his palm then lifted it with her skill and twirled it in the air before her. She studied it, each and every intricate little detail. "This bear looks exactly like you." She settled the bear in her palm and popped a kiss on its tiny head. "I shall treasure this gift. Thank you."

How he wished she'd pop a kiss on his head instead of his carving's. He clamped his lips shut for fear he'd utter his desire out loud.

"Is something wrong?" She looked at his tight lips, traced a finger over the lower one and he nipped her finger, sucked it into his mouth. Giggling, she plucked it free. "You have a very territorial bear."

"He's also hungry for you, and I'm struggling to keep myself from touching you."

"Well, the rabbit is almost done. That is the only meal your bear is allowed to eat, no' me."

The meaty aroma of their meal swirled all about and he removed the meat from the spit, set it to one side to cool down. "Tell me what your favorite food is." He longed to know everything about her, every little detail, no matter how big or small.

"Anything sweet. I adore honeyed plums and figs, lemon apple pie, and cherry tart. The cook makes these wonderful fruit pastries along with custard and cream." She nabbed her gown from beside her, tucked the figurine he'd made her into the pocket of the red velvet and set her gown back next to his belongings.

"We have what is called chocolate in my time, the most sensational sweet I've ever tasted."

"Oooh, chocolate. Even the name of it sounds decadent." She licked her pouty pink lips and he almost whimpered with his need to lick her lips too. "How do you make chocolate?"

"Ah…" He shoved his heady desire to lick her aside, tried to focus on her question. "I've no idea. I just know where to buy it."

"You buy your sweets?" Brows soaring, she wriggled closer, her knees touching his leg where he'd crossed them at the ankle.

"Aye, from a supermarket or a store." He'd love to drive

her into the local village near Ivanson Castle and take her shopping in the sweet section of the mall. There was even a dedicated shop in the village that sold various types of chocolates from all over the world. She'd never want to leave that store.

"Goodness, all this talk of food and sweets is making me very hungry." She rubbed her rumbling belly.

"Then let me feed my hungry mate." He checked the meat, found it had cooled well enough. After tearing the meat into small slivers, he held up a piece for her. "Come closer."

Wriggling closer and leaning in, she pressed her hand to his chest, right over his heart. "Is this close enough?"

"That's much better?" His heart skipped a beat then picked up its pace. Gently, he slipped the morsel between her lips, his bear clawing to get even closer to her, to tip her onto her back on the sand and trap her underneath him.

"This meat is delicious." She chewed, her hand still a hot brand against his skin as he fed her another morsel then took a bite for himself. Small steps. Those would be what he'd have to take in order to win the woman who held the other half of his soul to his side. Slowly but surely, he would woo her until she could no longer withhold herself from him. He certainly wouldn't be able to hold himself back from her for much longer. He continued to feed her, until she held up a hand and pleaded, "No more for me."

"Are you certain?"

"Very." She laid down on the sand, stretched with a smile of pure satisfaction, her gaze on the stars twinkling through the vent high above. "You finish the rest of the meal off."

He finished it, licked his fingers and stretched out beside her, the sand a soft mattress underneath him as he trailed one finger down her arm. "Would you like another swim?"

"I would, but mayhap in the morn." She yawned and curled onto her side as she faced him. "I'm tired. I rose early this morn since I had trouble sleeping last eve."

"I had trouble sleeping last night as well." Unease at being so far away from her had taken ahold of him and wouldn't let go. Even now, with her so close, she still remained too far from his touch. He longed to wrap his arms around her, tuck her in close against him and allow his scent and warmth to surround her.

Instead, he waited as she drifted toward sleep and counseled his bear that a slow yet sure pursuit would be needed with their chosen one. Aye, she'd asked for some time and he needed to give it to her, although he had no intention of allowing her to keep her distance for too long. He'd never survive it if he did.

* * * *

The early morning sunshine beamed through the vent high above and flickered across Layla's closed eyelids, while the steam swirling through their sacred cavern dampened her skin. From somewhere outside, birds twittered and she stretched, burrowed her nose deeper into firm flesh as the soul-satisfying scent of Tor surrounded her. Mmm, he smelled divine, like that of the outdoors, the sun and the sea and all that she adored about her homeland.

She lifted one eyelid and bit down on her lower lip. Nay, nay, nay. Her legs were tangled with his and she lay almost half over top of him, her hands bunched in his tunic and his warm breath fanning gently over her forehead. How had she ended up in this intimate position? She needed to move away, with all speed, except when she tried to release him, she instead spread her hands more fully over his solid chest.

His muscles flexed under her touch and she trailed one finger over the tight bands of muscle layered across this stomach under the thin white cotton. His midnight black hair caught the dawn's light and shimmered a fiery blue on the ends, the razz of stubble on his jaw giving him an early-morning, sensually-hot look that made her mouth water for more of him. Goodness. She shook her head. Turn away. Look anywhere but at him, because if she didn't, she'd touch him, and far more than she should considering her betrothed state.

She scuttled back, jumped to her feet, dashed into the warm water of the pool and dove. Kicking, she cut a fast path across the surface toward the overhanging ledge running alongside the wall at the far side. Hands planted on the ledge, she gave herself a push up with her skill and sat on top of the warm stone, feet dangling in the water.

"You moved fast just then." Tor stretched as he rose from the sand, shoved his black leather pants down his legs and with his white tunic fluttering against him mid-thigh, he bounded into the water. He dove and swam underneath, a wave rippling toward her and the streak of white which must be his shirt, shimmering just below the surface. He burst from the water in front of her, clamped one hand on her ankle and grinned. "Want to play?" He flashed a smile full of challenge then released her and backed away. "Or are you too wary to swim with a bear?"

"I'm wary of naught." She'd show him she could swim and play and not be perturbed in the least. "Race you to the other side." She stood and dove from the top of the overhanging ledge. Kicking, she swam hard and when he drew up alongside her, she sent a wave of water crashing into him with her skill and powered ahead.

He roared, plowed after her and caught her up as she touched the wall. He nabbed her around the waist and chuckled as he twirled her about in the water. "I love your form of play, sweet Layla, my challenging mate."

His wolfish gaze and his hands on her hips sent a thrill racing through her then gently, he lowered her down, sliding her along the length of his body as he did. She cleared her throat. "Let's race back to the other side."

"I'll give you a head-start." He released her. "No cheating this time."

"You are taller and stronger than me." Cheat she would.

She shoved another wave of water at him, tossed her feet in the air and went under. Swimming, she kicked, until her lungs were near to bursting then headed to the surface. Tor swam toward her on top and whizzed in front, his muscled legs strong and propelling him forward far faster than she could ever manage. She seized his feet as he flew by, held on as he powered them both to the ledge with sure strokes from his gloriously muscled arms alone.

With his hands on the rock, he hauled himself up, reached down and lifted her onto the flat stone next to him. Water sluiced down his legs and his laughter rang out and echoed all around. "I haven't had this much fun in ages."

"Neither have I, although we should return soon." She wrung out her long locks then picked up the trailing ends of her shift and squeezed the water from it. "Father and I always break our fast together. He'll know I'm missing afore too long."

"Then I thank you for spending the night with me." He caught her hand, pressed it against his thumping heartbeat. "I'll forever remember this day."

"So will I." Spreading her fingers over his flesh, she reveled in the heat he emitted. His wet tunic clung to his heavily muscled chest and a smattering of hair, as dark as his head, showed through the white linen. She slid one finger into the gap between the loosened ties of the V neckline then trailed down between the contoured planes of his belly. His rigid abs tightened under her touch and his heat blasted toward her, made her want to wriggle even closer. Oh, and now that she'd started touching him again, she couldn't stop. She swished along his trim waist, a raw and hungry need rearing to full and vibrant life within her. She wanted him, wanted more.

* * * *

Tor closed his eyes, opened them again and tried heartedly to get his racing heartbeat under control. Layla's breath came as hard and fast as his did, her brown eyes darkening to a hungry hue as she traced along his waist.

The white cotton of her wet shift, almost transparent where it pressed against her chest, showed the perfect fullness of her breasts and a mouthwatering tease of ruby pink nipple. The sight had his cock hardening and his need for her rearing with fierce intensity. He yearned for her touch, for her trust and her heart. She was his, just as he was hers.

Gently, he swept his hand around hers, brought her fingers to his lips and pressed a soft kiss against her palm. He nibbled up, along her wrist then rubbed his cheek against the creamy skin of her inner forearm. Being surrounded by her scent and ensuring she carried his own, consumed him. How he wished to bite her as their shifter kind did, to leave his mark on her so all others would know she was his, but instead he breathed slowly, forced the deep desire down and attempted to calm himself. Time. She'd asked for some time and as much as he hated giving it to her, he would.

"Are you all right, Tor?"

"I'll be fine. It's just that I need you."

"In what way?" She inched closer, sank one hand into his hair and lightly raked her nails over his scalp.

His bear rumbled deep inside him, her touch a mark of claim that brought such peace to his soul. He wanted her caressing all of him, her mouth on his neck and the ultimate mark of her claim made right there on his flesh for all to see. "I want to bite you, for you to bite me." He looked deep into her eyes. "You're my mate and no other's. I'll never give you up."

"You are stealing my will to be anywhere but here with you." She wriggled her fingers free of his, shoved her hands in her lap then stared at her whitened knuckles. "What kind of a woman promises herself to one man then so readily touches another?"

"Don't. I adore your touch, need it to the depths of my soul and I've no doubt my need calls to yours, increases and inflames it. It hurts when you pull away." With one finger under her chin, he lifted her gaze back to his then traced his thumbs over the dusting of freckles smattered across her tiny nose and cheeks. "Touch me, as freely as you wish. I'm yours, always and forever."

"This bond is so all-consuming."

"Aye, but in a very good way." He pushed to his feet and lifted her to hers. She needed a moment to relax again, to not worry about their bond and the depth it raged. She enjoyed playing and so did he. He'd play with her some more. He swept her up into his arms then tossed her into the water with a resounding splash and dove in after her.

She emerged, spluttering and laughing just as he did, her long hair floating like a silken web of gold around her as she treaded water. "Your bear is far too playful for me right now."

"Do you wish to head in?" He tipped his head toward the beach. "Or take me on once more? I know you can."

"I would adore taking you on, but I'm afraid we should return afore a search party is dispatched. I've no wish for anyone else to discover this sacred place. It is ours alone." She swam in and once her feet touched the ground, she slogged through the water to the sandy shore.

He set out after her, kicked into shore and joined her on the beach then wrung his shirt out as best as he could, although it'd dry quick enough since his temperature ran hotter than most. All shifters' blood did.

Gripping the hem of her sopping shift, she eyed him. "I need to remove this undergarment. The wet cotton will chaff my skin if I wear it underneath my gown. Could you turn around?"

"I'd rather not." Except he did, giving her the privacy she'd asked for. He shook the sand from his black pants and jammed them on, fastened his sword belt and tugged on his boots. Done, he waited, rested one hand on the warm surface of the damp rock wall. "Let me know when you're dressed."

"I still need a moment." A wet plop, the swish of velvet falling in a whoosh then her soft step as she moved across the sand toward the fire pit. "Now I'm done."

He turned around, his pulse racing at the way she smiled at him, her brown eyes dancing with mischief and her lush lips lifted with a sultry sensuality he longed to taste for himself. "It's time to leave."

"Aye, it is." She knelt before the fire and even though it had died out some hours ago, she scooped sand and tossed it over the charred remains to ensure not even a spark remained alight. She rose, picked up the cane basket of cherries in one hand and tucked her wet shift inside it, her shawl again draped over her shoulders. "What are your plans for the day, Tor?"

"To speak to your father and then my brother. I need to inform them both that I've found my chosen one and that she is you. Following that, I intend to continue wooing you."

"Do you have another hidden pool to show me?" Grinning mischievously, she wandered toward the tunnel's entrance and sent the basket floating ahead of her down the darkened passageway. She bounded up onto the rock, her red skirts clinging to her pert bottom and her hips swaying so enticingly as she sashayed out of his sight.

His bear growled deep inside him, doubling his demand for her. Hell, keeping his hands off her until she'd ended her betrothal would be one of the hardest things he'd ever done. He lengthened his stride, caught up with her as she squeezed through the thinning gap at the end of the stone ledge and joined her outside, the crashing of the waterfall and life beyond their secret haven, resounding all around.

"This place is so enchanting." She pressed herself against the mist-covered rock wall, the clear sheet of water arching over them and pounding into the pool nestled within the ravine far below. The morning sunshine beamed bright, flared through the cascading water and sent a colorful rainbow of beautiful yellows, pinks, reds and blues shimmering over her upturned face.

"You're the enchanting one." Her beauty was one of sweet, youthful innocence, her vibrant love for her clan making her glow all the more and drawing him in. Unable to help himself, he traced his knuckles gently down the softness of her cheek, her flawless skin warm to the touch. He dropped a kiss on the tip of her tiny nose, wanted to smother her face in a myriad of kisses. "You'll need to set the basket down on the other side of the ledge, Layla."

"Why?"

"So you don't drop it when I kiss you proper."

"There shall be no kissing." She tapped his chest. "None whatsoever."

"I keep telling myself not to touch you, to give you the time you've asked for, but I'm struggling to adhere to your request." He gave her his most hopeful expression. "Please, surely one kiss wouldn't hurt."

"One kiss will likely lead to so much more, and you are a terrible tease for even asking." Giggling, she floated the basket toward the grassy cliff side. "And I am no' setting this basket down so you can kiss me, in case it appeared that way."

"You are a very mean mate." He followed her along the ledge where the view opened up then breathed deep as he took in the beauty of the land spread out before them. At the bottom of the hills, the House of Clan Matheson rose like a sentinel, the inner channel of Loch Alsh weaving inland like a ribbon of blue silk, while across the sea's choppy ocean waves to the west, the northern tip of the Isle of Skye rose with a layer of white cloud swelling over it. Skye. Clan MacDonald's land, and that of his mate's betrothed. He edged past her on the ledge, bounded onto the grassy bank and arms extended, nodded. "Jump."

She took a step back then bounded across.

He caught her, twirled her around onto his other side and safely away the sheer cliff edge.

"Oh my." Laughing, she spun about, her damp blond locks streaming behind her and her rosy cheeks and smile so captivating. "Never have I felt so free as I do in this moment."

In a way, neither had he, no matter he had Donnan MacDonald still to contend with. His woman had certainly cast a spell over him, fully and completely ensnaring him and he wanted it no other way. Her brown eyes, as rich in color as dark chocolate, sparkled with vigor and vitality and his desire to hold her close, roared through him with thundering need. He'd get no respite from that need, not for the rest of his life. The one woman he desired to spend the rest of his days with stood before him and all he wanted to do was fall to his knees then take her down with him and worship her body.

"Thank you for bringing me here, to this most precious place." She closed the distance between them, pressed one hand against his chest, right over his heart as she reached up on her toes and kissed his chin.

"This will be our place, only yours and mine, always and forever." He slid one hand over her hip and the other around to the small of her back. "By the way, you missed my mouth by an inch. Are you certain I cannae claim a kiss?"

"Positive."

"My bear is feeling incredibly territorial right now." He dipped his head, rubbed his cheek against her cheek and embedded more of his scent into her flesh.

"Can you control him?" She curved her body into his, her hips rubbing against his hips.

"Barely. He wants you to desire us, the same way that we desire you." He nuzzled her neck, scraped his teeth along the sensitive hollow where her shoulder and neck met and she dug her fingers into his biceps and held on piercingly tight.

"I do desire both of you. Never think I dinnae." Panting, she pulled back an inch, her chest heaving within the constraints of her low-cut bodice, her full breasts swelling forth. "You muddle my thoughts, make me lose my mind when you're this close."

"Muddling is good." He wanted his mate, but for her to come to him freely. Slowly, he slid his hands down her sides, stepped back and picked up the basket. Time for them to leave this place before he no longer could. "You lead the way down the trail. I need to speak to your father and my brother, as soon as possible."

"Father will be quite shocked to learn I'm now mated. He waited three years from my coming of age to ensure I wasnae." She grasped her deep red skirts and glided down the winding forest trail, her long golden locks swaying at her waist, strands lifting and fluttering as they dried in the gentle breeze.

Down the forest pathway thick either side with low scrub, he followed his chosen one, as he'd follow her anywhere their lives led them. Small creatures rustled within the undergrowth while in the canopy high above, birds twittered within their nests. The air swirled and Layla's wild cherry scent wafted over him, so fresh and sweet and beyond tempting. All he wanted to do was catch her up in his arms, tramp right back up that trail to their hidden pool and have his wicked way with her. She was his mate, the one woman he would lay his life down for, never wished to be without, never—

"'Tis so peaceful here. Dinnae you think so, Tor?" She skipped over thick tree roots twisting across the path, turned and bounced backward, her smile wide.

"Watch your step."

"You need only watch your own—" She stumbled over a snaking root and gasped, toppled back and caught herself midair. Floating a few inches above the ground, her hair brushing the grassy trail, she seized the basket he'd dropped as he'd launched himself to catch her, the spill of cherries bobbing in the air as he gripped her around the waist. They floated just like that, him stretched out over top of her, every inch of their bodies touching.

Weightless, he arched a brow at her. "You were saying…"

"Step. You need only watch your own step and never mind mine. I've yet to topple over and not catch myself in time as I just did." Gently, she touched a finger to his lower lip. "I do wonder what it would be like to kiss you. I want you to know that."

"I want to do far more than kiss you right now. I want to devour you."

"Our mated bond is growing swiftly."

"Aye, the ties binding our souls together will continue to weave into one until not a single strand separates us." He closed his eyes, opened them again, his very essence demanding he take the choice from her, kiss her and never let her go. Although the man his father had taught him to be, made him remain right where he was. "I want you, heart, body, and soul."

"You have already stolen a piece of my heart, a piece I'll never be able to claim back again." She pushed her hands into his hair, buried her face in his neck then lifted them up with her skill and set them back down on their feet. She stepped back, swept the floating cherries into the basket and motioned for him to take it. "'Tis all yours again. Dinnae drop the basket again."

"Thank you."

With a soft sigh, she continued on down the path, her next softly whispered words floating to him. "I'm sorry."

"You've no need to be sorry." He trekked after her and before too long, they emerged from the woods and the thick stone walls of the House of Clan Matheson rose like an impenetrable fortress. Guardsmen patrolled the battlements either side of the gatehouse, while the four-story north tower house beyond it overlooked it all. Clear skies reigned overhead with only a smattering of gauzy white cloud and the sun, a fiery burst of golden-yellow, spread its summer warmth across their land.

At the sea-gate, the glittering waters of the loch lapped gently into shore and near the stables, a gangly-legged lad in loosely belted breeches brushed a sleek black war horse while next to him, two armed warriors mounted their steeds then galloped past and disappeared down the main trail into the depths of the forest.

They walked underneath the gate's arch and inside the keep. Across the inner bailey in the training area, a good fifty warriors wielded swords in a battle of strength against one another, Tavish and Kirk amongst them.

"Father." Layla lifted a hand as Gregor strode toward them in a loose tan tunic over his belted plaid, his sword swinging at his side and his dark hair cut short, a streak of silver flaring back from his brow on one side.

"I was just about to ride out and search for you." Gregor caught Layla up in his arms and hugged her, his love for his daughter shining through. "Have you been out all night?"

"Aye." A flush bloomed on her cheeks. "Tor and I are mated, Father. We discovered the bond had taken when the full moon rose."

"You're mated to Tor?" Gregor shot him a wide-eyed look. "Is this true? Your chosen one is my daughter?"

"Layla is the one both me and my bear were directly led to, although of course we've hit a snag considering her betrothal."

"Damn it." Gregor groaned, slapped a hand against his forehead. "I waited three years after she came of age to make certain she wasnae soul bound to another as so many of our fae kind are. Donnan will be furious to hear this news. He glanced at his daughter, his gaze softening. "What is your intention?"

"I made a vow to Donnan, and I've no wish to forsake my duty to my clan, but so too I sense the strength of my bond forming with Tor and 'tis unmistakable."

"Which means your duty to your clan is now twofold. We have a need to cement the ties between us and clan MacDonald, but there is also our clan's need to ensure Gilleoin's future shifter line does no' fall into extinction. The 'Son of the Bear' cannae be allowed to falter." Gregor gripped Layla's shoulders. "Do you wish to accept the bond?"

"I dinnae know how to make things right with Donnan if I do." She glanced at Tor over her shoulder. "I've asked my mate for some time so I might be able to, well, sort everything out in my mind."

Tor handed her the basket. "Why don't you go inside, take the cherries to the cook and take some time to think things through now. I'll speak to your father while you do, and try not to fret."

"You'll come and find me afterward?" She tightened her grip on the basket, held it firm against her chest.

"Of course. You're my mate, always mine and I'll never be too far away from you." He would fight for her, take on Donnan MacDonald and ensure the man knew that Layla was his. "I'll see you soon."

"Aye, soon." She walked inside, disappeared through the double paneled front doors holding the carved image of their clan chief's crest emblazoned on the front. The chief's arms held two bears as supporters either side, those bears signifying all that they fought for—the survival of a loyal race of bear shifters—Gilleoin's line, his clan's line. Layla was his one true mate and they must continue to grow from strength to strength together. Never apart.

With every step Layla took away from him, his heart heaved and his very soul wrenched with pain. He rubbed his achy chest and grimaced. "It's not easy having her leave."

"I remember the pain well." Solemn words and an equally solemn nod from Gregor. "These past three years have been difficult for Layla. As much as our fae people long to have a soul bound mate, my daughter has in her own way feared it, whether she wished for me to see that fear or no', I did. She has no wish to suffer the pain of losing her chosen one as I lost her mother."

"She will never lose me." He clasped Gregor's shoulder.

“I'll fight for her.”

“I dinnae doubt you will.”

Chapter 3

Layla entered the great hall, her thoughts in turmoil as she passed the blazing fireplace with their clan shield glimmering in its rightful place above it. Her duty was twofold, to ensuring Gilleoin's future shifter line didn't fall into extinction, and also to honoring her betrothal agreement with Donnan. She sank down on a bench at one of the trestle tables now cleared of the morning meal, set her basket of cherries on the seat beside her and rubbed her tight chest, her heart a heavy weight within it. Her soul bond with Tor resonated strongly within her, her need for him growing with each hour that passed. Spending the night with him in their sacred cavern had been so enchanting, so beautiful, and even though he was only a short distance away, her heart still called to his and her very soul resonated with need.

"Good morn, my lady." Effie, one of the maids, walked across the hall tucking one errant lock of her hair underneath her frilly white cap. "Would you like me to bring a tray up to your chamber? I'm fetching one for Cherub and can do so for you too."

"I would love one, thank you. I've yet to break my fast. I take it Cherub's in her chamber?"

"She is. I'll take these cherries to the cook for you as well, bring you both a tray once I'm done. I willnae be long." Effie scooped up the basket and disappeared around the edge of the great hall toward the kitchens.

"Layla!" Cherub waved out as she skipped down the last step of the stairwell, her flawless skin sparkling, just like that of the stars she moved amongst when traveling through time. "I saw you arrive back while at my window."

"I have news." She hurried across to Cherub, grasped her hands. "Tor and I are mated."

"I gathered as such. When the full moon rose, I finally sensed who it was Tor had been searching for. You." Smiling wide, Cherub twirled her in a circle, the burgundy ribbons looped around the waist of her corseted cream gown rippling and her white hooded cloak fluttering from her shoulders. "'Tis good to see you're no longer in hiding from him."

"I didnae realize I was hiding from him. I also cannae believe we're mated when I'm betrothed to another."

"Aye, your betrothal does pose an issue, but 'tis naught we cannae fix."

"Tor's speaking to Father now. Already I miss him, although I've asked Tor for some time to consider things. I dinnae know quite what to do. All I know is that he is the only one I will ever desire."

"Come then. Let's talk in your chamber where we cannae be overheard." Cherub hooked her arm through hers and led her toward the stairwell.

"I hope you hold the answer to my questions, or at least some solid guidance. I'm in desperate need of it this day." She scaled the stairs to the second floor and traversed down the corridor lit by a hazy beam of sunshine streaming through the narrow window at the far end. At the fourth chamber on the left, she opened the thickly paneled door and motioned Cherub inside. "Take a seat while I change. I willnae be long."

"Take as long as you need." Cherub sat at the side table,

fluffed her skirts about her.

Quickly, she crossed to her burgundy curtained ambry and selected a change of clothes, a rich royal blue gown with long sleeves edged in white lace that draped over the backs of her hands. She always wore it donned with her mother's favorite leather girdle embellished with bits of bronze. Father had gifted the heirloom to her when she'd come of age, along with a few of her mother's other most beloved trinkets. She dug Nessa's missive out of her pocket along with the bear figurine, kissed the top of the bear's head and popped the carving and the folded parchment inside her wooden keepsake box. She'd forever cherish the memento Tor had given her, as well as Nessa's precious words. That poem would remain etched within her heart for all time.

"Here we are." Effie arrived with a tray holding a teapot and two cups, oatcakes and raspberry tarts for both her and Cherub.

"I'll take my tea here with Layla, rather than in my chamber. Thank you, Effie." Cherub moved a red leather-bound book out of the way and patted the tabletop.

Her maid set the tray on the embroidered cloth in the center then closed the door behind her as she left.

With her blue gown in hand, Layla nipped in behind the corner dressing screen hand-painted with rolling moors awash with purple heather.

"Do you have honey in your tea?" Cherub called out.

"Aye, a good spoonful. I like it sweet." She shed her clothes, donned a clean ivory shift then tugged her gown over her head. The whisper-soft velvet shimmered over her hips and swished to her ankles. She adjusted the scalloped neckline with its pretty embroidered white-lace edging that draped low along her neckline, belted her mother's precious girdle about her waist and slid her feet into a pair of matching royal blue slippers. Dressed, she nabbed her comb from the table holding a basin and jug and in the looking glass, ran the comb through her spiral locks until she'd tamed them once more.

"Tell me all about the moment when Tor discovered you two were soul bound." Cherub stirred honey into the tea. "I cannae wait to hear of all that happened."

"He sensed the bond taking form between us even afore night had fallen. I picked the cherries then he asked me to join him for a swim. He said he wished to show me a sacred cavern he'd found hidden behind the waterfall high in the hills, one that held a warm pool of water, then he carted me off up the hill even though I'd said I couldnae come." From her dish holding a spill of ribbons, she selected a circlet headband of red silk flowers with trailing red and white ribbons and popped it on top of her head to keep her curls in place. 'Twas the same headband she'd worn the day Tor had arrived in their time, the day she'd first met him. A smile came to her lips. The memory of their first meeting would always hold a special place in her heart, as would the night before in their most special place.

"Did you stay in the cavern for the night?" Cherub enquired.

"Aye, we did." She sat at the side table opposite Cherub. "While he carted me up the hill, he asked me what I was hiding, but I swore I hid naught."

"The fact you are betrothed to another man must have been what caused him to miss the earlier signs of your bond taking form. In a way, you were hiding."

"The day he first arrived in this time, he told me once he'd learned I was betrothed to another, the knowledge had frustrated him and in all honesty, I've always felt far more than mere intrigue alone for him. I simply wasnae willing to acknowledge it, no' to myself or to any other."

"What happened next?" Cherub nudged her tea cup toward her. "Once you arrived at the cavern."

"We swam, and as the sun descended and the full moon

rose, he shifted and allowed me to pet his bear. When he shifted back, he gave me his oath. He vowed that whatever path I trod, would be the same path that he did and he offered me his full protection, of all that he is. He insisted he'd always be here, fighting for me."

"His need to complete the bond and join in all ways will be surging strongly through him now that he knows you're his." Cherub munched on an oatcake, her blond locks sliding over her shoulder and shimmering bright.

"Aye, he asked for a courtship, and I agreed, but there truly is little I can do about allowing anymore between us until I've spoken to Donnan. He is the one to whom I've agreed to wed."

"I understand." Cherub arched a brow. "Although dinnae forget Nessa's words."

"I never could, no' now." She lifted her tea cup and sipped the sweet brew, her thoughts rolling around in turmoil. "Three years ago, when I first discovered I wasnae mated to another of my fae kind, I was quietly relieved. I've always believed 'tis better to be wed to a man I have no feelings for than to ever worry over losing the one man I can never live without."

"Yet Tor willnae be able to live without you should you choose Donnan over him." Cherub cleared her throat, her gaze intent. "If you choose to deny your bond with Tor, then you'd be forcing him to live as your father has lived these past twenty-three years, without the one woman his very heart and soul cries out for. *Dinnae cast aside that which is freely given, for your happiness is all I seek.*" Cherub recited Nessa's words, ones that touched her heart. "The bond is freely given, Layla."

"The bond is also all-consuming."

"Aye, but in a very good way." Cherub's face lit up with a silly smile then she frowned. "And also in a very frustrating way, but still, I wouldnae wish to be without my mate. Kirk stands at my side, just as I stand at his. My duty to my fae people has now become his duty too and I could never live without him, would perish if I did."

"'Tis the living without that I fear." She selected one of the gooey raspberry tarts and chewed.

"Tor's been searching for you for such a long time." Cherub patted her hand. "I understand your fears, but he will never be complete until the two of you have joined together as one. You must sever your ties to Donnan then allow the bond to take. Accept your destiny and embrace your new future. *The fates do speak and now is your time,* as Nessa said. Open your heart to your mate, Layla, and I promise that you'll never regret doing so." Cherub motioned toward the open window where the clanging of steel and the grunting of warriors at training ricocheted toward them. "Tor will be lost without you. You are his destiny, just as he is yours, and if you take but one step toward him, he'll be there to hold you. So either you accept that the fates have brought you two together, or you toss all that could be away and lose your heart's true desire."

"I cannae deny I want him."

"A MacDonald galley approaches!" The corner guardsman's booming voice filtered through, ringing with authority from the ramparts overlooking the loch.

Layla raced to the window and grasped the stone windowsill. A galley bearing a MacDonald flag on the center mast confirmed the arrival of their allied clan. At the helm, with a mighty two-handed claymore holstered across his back, Donnan MacDonald stood, his biceps bulging and his legs spread wide. No one could mistake the Chief of MacDonald's son, and certainly not her. He was the man she'd spent time with on Skye, the man she'd not sensed one inkling of desire for, and the one man she could safely wed and never fear any heartache over losing. He was her betrothed.

"I'll go and see if Kirk needs my aid now that we have guests soon arriving." Cherub squeezed her shoulder. "Think on all we've spoken about and if you need to talk to me further, I'll always be here."

"Thank you, Cherub. I shall take your wise advice and Nessa's words too, to heart."

"Then that is all either your godmother or I could ask of you." Cherub dissolved into a mist and streamed out the window and retook her form near the gate as Kirk jogged across the yard and joined her. Cherub pulled her white cape's fur hood over her head and wandered out the gate arm-and-arm with her mate. The Fae Angel of Love always took great care with whom she allowed to see her, her cloak and hood fully protecting her identity. She wouldn't be exposing her true self to their visitors, but so too she would remain near Kirk while he welcomed Donnan and his men.

Near the battling warriors training below, Tor stood next to Tavish, both brothers identical in every way, from their shoulder-length locks of silky black hair to their broad chests and towering height, although she'd never mistake one for the other, not now. Using her skill, she swished the wind and brought Tor and Tavish's conversation to her.

"They're set to wed before the end of the week." Tor blew out a long breath, fists clenching and unclenching at his sides. "No one takes Layla from me, not now, not ever."

"I won't allow you to lose her either. Whatever you need me to do, I'll do." Tavish made the promise with complete ease, their brotherly bond so very tight.

"All I wish to do is protect her from what is about to happen, because breaking the allied relationship between the clans isn't what I'm after, only breaking her betrothal is." Tor slid one hand into his pants pocket and dug out the red ribbon he'd taken from her, his gaze softening as he wound it around one finger. "I also won't take her away from her loved ones here. She needs her father."

"As Julia needs her parents. We travel back and forth as needed. Cherub would do the same for you and Layla." Tavish touched his sword to Tor's sheathed one. "Train with me. You're strung with tension and need to release it."

Tor pocketed her ribbon, slid his blade free of his side scabbard and in a series of smooth moves, warmed up. "Once I've cleared my head, I intend to tackle my challenging mate, then I'll deal with Donnan. I won't have her anywhere near him while he and his clansmen visit."

"A sound idea."

"I'll need your aid in watching over her." Tor slammed his blade into Tavish's, his biceps flexing and his tunic pulled taut across his broad shoulders. She curled her fingers into the sill, her need to touch him, to hold him, to never let him go rolling swiftly through her. He battled hard, sweat dampening his skin and as he met each and every one of Tavish's fast and deadly strikes, the hem of his billowy white tunic lifted and gave her a stunning glimpse of his tapered waist and trim hips. She wished to see more of him, could barely contain the need.

With one thought alone, she tore his shirt from him and the scraps of linen swept across the stony yard in the breeze and fluttered against the curtain wall. Tor halted, shock coursing across his face. Oh goodness. She clasped a hand to her mouth. Had she really done that?

Tor glanced toward her window, caught sight of her, his golden shifter gaze locking tight with hers and every delicious inch of his chest now hers for the viewing. Cherub had said if she but opened her heart to him, she'd never regret it and already she struggled to keep Tor at arm's reach, her need to touch him a constant burn in her blood. Her mouth watered as she ogled his firm abs and tanned pecs. That teasing trail of dark hair that disappeared below the waistband of his leather pants, made her chest tighten with need.

"It looks like your time is already up." Tavish slapped Tor's shoulder. "I believe you're needed elsewhere."

"Aye, and with all haste." Tor sheathed his sword and

jogged toward the front door.

Heat flushed her cheeks and mortified, she dropped her face into her hands. Well, she'd certainly promised Cherub she'd consider her advice and it seemed she had. She was mated to a shifter and that mate would be here very soon.

"Layla?" A knock rattled the door. "I need to come in."

"Nay."

"Wrong answer." Tor strode in and shut the door behind him, his chest heaving from his fast run. He slid the bolt home, his gaze roaming over her then he crooked one finger. "Come here, my challenging mate."

"I'm sorry. I didnae mean to rip your tunic from you."

"Never say sorry for undressing me, although I'd rather you do so in private, but for now, I'll take whatever you're willing to offer." He crooked his finger again. "Come closer…if you dare."

"I heard your conversation below in the yard with Tavish. Cherub and I too have spoken." She rolled her shoulders and straightened her back. She could do this. 'Twas time to show her mate exactly what he meant to her.

"About…" A world of encouragement graced that one word.

"Cherub said you're my match in every way, and if I but open my heart to you, I'll never regret it. She said you'd be lost without me, never at peace unless I allowed the bond. You are my destiny, just as I am yours, and if I take but one step toward you, you'll be there to hold me." She pushed one foot forward, then the next.

"She's damn right." He waited, his gaze not straying from her.

"So either I accept that the fates have brought us both together, or I toss all that could be aside and lose my heart's true desire." She halted in front of him and he gripped her waist, his hands so big and warm and sending a thrill jolting through her. "I cannae deny I want you. Being near you excites me, soothes me, and that desire consumes my very soul."

"Keep talking. This conversation is currently headed in the right direction." He dipped his head, touched his forehead to hers. "You are my mate, the only woman I'll ever desire, my match in every way. I'll speak to Donnan, at the first possible opportunity. Ensure he knows there will be no marriage between the two of you."

"Nay, I need to be the one to speak to him."

"That's not happening." He stroked around to her bottom, squeezed her rear through the mountainous folds of royal blue velvet and rubbed his body against hers. "I don't want you anywhere near Donnan. My bear is clawing to keep you by our side, and right now I need to smother you in my scent, bite you, lick you, and anything else you'll permit."

"We cannae complete the bond until I've spoken to Donnan and I'm no longer betrothed to him. The guilt would consume me otherwise." She wrapped her arms around his neck, raked her nails lightly down the length of his golden skinned back. "You're my bear, my mate, my fierce steward."

"Do that again, but harder, and that's an order." He swung her around, pressed her back against the door, his body a hot flare of heat that surrounded her. "My bear's rumbling for more."

"'Tis best I warn you then that I'm terrible at following orders." She lightly swished her fingers down his chest and along his trim waist. "Always have been and always will be."

"I can tell." He trailed one finger along the upper swells of her breasts exposed by the scalloped neckline. Licking his lips, he leaned in then buried his nose in the valley of her breasts. "You smell so wildly sweet."

"Kiss me." She caught his face in her hands, lifted his gaze back to hers. "No more do I intend to withhold myself from you."

"You're certain?"

"Kiss me."

"Thank you." He dipped his head, covered her mouth with his and took her breath away with a scorching kiss, one that made her sway into him, his hard body pressed into hers and blazing with heat. He licked across her tongue and she melted into him, reveling in his fresh outdoor scent, that of the sun and the sea and the wilds of her homeland. His delicious scent swirled all around and embedded itself deeply within her. How could she have ever thought she might turn away from him and accept another? Not for a moment could she have done so.

"More," she demanded.

"Aye, more." His breath whispered across her tongue, a sensuous caress that had her urging his lips farther apart to deepen their kiss.

Naught had ever felt so right and she indulged in her need for him, plunged her tongue inside his mouth and drank in his wickedly hot taste. She craved this raw intimacy, desired him and only him. "Tor," she panted, pulling back a touch. "I'm about to lose myself."

"Perfect, because I want you to get lost in me." He caressed her sides, roamed down and scooped her bottom up then lifted her and carried her to her bed. He kissed her again as he laid her down on the soft bedcovers and moved in over top of her, his kiss deep, wild and completely untamed, their breath mingling as one and scattering every one of her thoughts.

"Mark me, just as your shifter kind do." A panting, needy request. "Please, Tor."

"My bite will be visible to one and all. It can be no other way." A deep purr rumbled from him as he nibbled along her jaw then followed the smooth line of her neck down to where her shoulder and neck met. He ran this thumb in a soothing swirl over her rapidly beating pulse point. "Right here is where I wish to mark you, although it's not the only place."

"Where else?"

"Right here." He swept his thumb along the top rise of her breasts then smoothed down her body and gripped the hem of her gown. He flipped the velvet up, and looking into her eyes, caressed up her leg before gently easing her knees apart and stroking along the sensitive skin of her inner thighs, first one side and then the other. "Here as well."

"You truly do have a territorial bear."

"Aye, are you ready?"

"I'm—" He dipped his head, sucked on her neck and scraped his teeth over the sensitive skin. "Ready."

"So am I, beyond ready." He pressed his entire length of his body against hers, teased his tongue over her neck and slid one finger under the shoulder of her gown and eased the velvet down her arm. A low rumble vibrated in his chest and made her arch her back and press more fully into him, her only need that of experiencing even more of his exquisite touch.

"Bite me. I cannae wait any longer." Her heartbeat thumped and raced so fast.

"I never want to forget this moment." He curved his palm around her exposed breast, flicked her peaked nipple then bit down on her neck.

Arousal hit her hard and fast, swept her away on its rampaging wave. She clutched his bare shoulders, her nails digging into his flesh then she scraped down his back. No more denial. She'd give him what he wanted, just as she too would take what she now needed.

"Are you all right?" He licked her skin, soothing the spot he'd just bitten. "Your skin is so flushed."

"More. I tingle, everywhere. Give me more."

"I really like this suddenly compliant side of you." He rolled onto his side next to her then pulled her flush up against him, his hand firm on her thigh as he tucked his top leg between both of her legs, her skirts still rucked up between them and their bodies touching along their entire length. Slowly, he slid her hair back from her shoulder and eased the fabric of her gown down her other arm until both her breasts were bared to his ravenous gaze. "When a shifter bites his mate and his mate bites him, not only is it a mark of claim, but it's also an aphrodisiac to both the giver and the receiver." His hungry gaze roamed over her breasts. "Our bite excites sexual desire, which is why we only ever mark our chosen ones."

"So when I bite you, you will feel the same flood of desire that just consumed me?"

"I'm already flooded with desire for you. If you bite me, I might not be able to control myself and since you've asked that we hold off on completing the bond until you've broken your betrothal, then you'd best wait and bite me only when you're ready to join together in all ways."

She smoothed one thumb over his neck and his heavily beating pulse. Warmth rippled through her, heating her all over. "I will be biting you. Now."

"I just said—"

"I'm no' good at following orders, remember?" She licked across his neck, sucked his skin into her mouth and razzed his flesh with her teeth. Her nipples hardened into fiercely tight points and she rubbed her breasts against his hot chest to ease the discomfort, except it only seemed to heighten her need even more. "Are you ready?"

"Aye," he growled as he slid one hand around the back of her head to hold her mouth against him. "Bite me."

"Thank you." She sank her teeth into him and he clamped his teeth down onto the other side of her neck. A bolt of pleasure coursed through her, swept her away on an avalanche of need. He was hers and she wanted everyone to know it and this mark she'd given him would ensure it.

"Layla, so good," he hissed and rubbed his leg higher between hers.

"Tor," she murmured, her desperate need for him raging

even stronger. She'd been a fool to think for even one minute that she'd ever have been able to turn away from him.

"What do you want? Tell me and I'll see to it."

"I dinnae know. Bite me again. Touch me as you please. Just give me more. I need more."

"I understand." Gripping her bare thigh, his fingers firm on her flesh, he pressed his leg even higher against her entrance below and the sweet pressure had her moaning. "I've got you, my love." He urged her to move on him. "Let go as you please."

"Oh my." The friction against her nub was sublime. She rubbed against him, seeking something beyond her grasp even though she knew not what. Dizzy with desire, she kissed him, with all the hunger and intensity rolling through her and he kissed her back.

"Give yourself to me. I promise to look after you." He nipped down her neck, licked the first mark he'd given her then scraped his stubbly jaw along the tops of her breasts. He nipped and sucked at her flesh, dotting little bites all over both mounds before he drifted lower and edged down to the end of the bed.

His head disappeared under the folds of her skirts and even though she should be shocked, that emotion didn't even flare to life within her. He was her mate and her body was his, just as his body was hers.

She gasped as he nibbled along her inner thighs, staking his claim and marking her, his hot breath a heavenly flutter across her lower folds.

"I'll be gentle." Softly whispered words as he swept one finger over her nub.

White-hot pleasure hit her, so swiftly, so completely. It sent her soaring from her body and a bright array of colors sizzled behind her closed eyelids as she flew.

Slowly, she came back down, her hands in his hair, fingers digging into his scalp. "Oh my, you are one very, very clever bear."

"You liked my touch?"

"Immensely." Panting, she tried to get her heartbeat back into order. "Come here, Tor. Kiss me again."

* * * *

"I'm coming." Tor gently nipped along Layla's inner thigh, then the tops of her heaving breasts as he slid up her body. The last thing he wished to do was leave that heavenly spot between her legs where the heightened scent of her arousal had near made him come in his own pants. Watching her soar to the heavens from the touch of his finger alone had made both him and his bear deliriously happy and also incredibly fevered for more. He moaned as he gripped the burgundy and white patterned bedcovers either side of her head. If he let go, he'd tear her gown fully from her. As it was, her luscious breasts heaved as she still grappled for breath and her rosy nipples begged for his touch. He needed a taste of those sweet morsels, now.

"Are you hurting?" She blinked her eyes open, her beautiful brown eyes dazed.

"No, why would you ask?"

"You just whimpered as if hurt."

"I'm struggling to hold back." She was so responsive to his touch and he couldn't have asked for anything more.

"So I see." In a slow circle, she rubbed the spot on her neck where he'd first bitten her then palmed the mark and held it close. "No more biting me though. I'm no' sure if I can handle another episode like that without first tearing the rest of your clothes off you."

"That was hardly a warning if that was your intention. My cock is throbbing for release." He'd never touched a woman the way he'd touched her, never had sex since his shifter kind always waited for their mate, but he'd certainly watched a few interesting movies which had enlightened him to the act of lovemaking. Right now all he wanted to do was strip every last piece of clothing from her, return to the sweet juncture between her thighs and feast on that part of her weeping for him.

"Is there aught more I can do to aid you in your release, as you did for me?" She stroked down his sides and caressed his shaft through his leather pants. "I would hate for you to be in pain."

"I can handle the pain. I need to kiss you again." He cupped her face in his hands and kissed her, moved his mouth over hers in a slow exploration that left them both ragged for breath when he pulled back. "When I come for the first time, it'll be deep inside your body, right where I belong."

"Is that so?" She smiled, so mischievously he didn't doubt she would continue to tease him this mercilessly for the rest of his life. It was one life he couldn't wait to live. Aye, he'd found his mate and now his soul rejoiced that they'd soon be one. "What are you thinking that has that intriguing smile on your face?" she murmured against his ear.

"My soul is rejoicing at being with you."

"As mine is at being with you. You are the only man I ever want touching me, and after what you just did to me, I see the error of my ways. I should never have questioned whether or not I'd accept the bond. I shall, with all of my heart."

"Those are the most beautiful words I've ever heard." He grinned, beyond taken by the woman who was his. Well, almost his. Once her betrothal was broken, he would lay claim to every last inch of her. She would be his wife, not Donnan MacDonald's.

Chapter 4

Before Tor lost all thought and took his mate just as he wished to, he instead lifted her bodice back over her breasts, righted her skirts and forced himself to rise from her bed. "I want you to stay right here."

"Where are you going?" She sat up, her beautiful golden curls mussed and the circlet headband of red silk flowers with trailing red and white ribbons now completely askew. She appeared a vision in her royal blue gown with its lacy white embroidered scalloped neckline, cinched waist and leather girdle with blue tasseled ties draping down to her knees. All he wanted to do was climb back into bed with her and never leave her again.

"To my chamber to collect my belongings. I'll pack what I need to and return. From now on, I sleep in here with you." He strode to her door, unbolted and opened it. "I'll also wash up and change since I'm already without a shirt. Give me ten minutes."

"I'll be waiting." She grinned, her gaze roaming his body and halting with mischievous intent on his crotch. "Particularly since I enjoy your attention so well."

"You're a vixen." He fixed his too tight pants.

"Aye, but I'm now your vixen."

"No moving. Stay right there on that bed." He closed her door then gathered his scrambled thoughts and strode down the corridor with its narrow window at the end emitting a stream of midday sunshine.

In his chamber, he shucked his clothes, donned a clean pair of pants in a soft, faded brown leather and tucked her red ribbon from the old pair into the pocket of his new ones. He chose a loose-sleeved black shirt with golden thread sewn in a circular Celtic belted design on the front pocket. The design surrounded a tiny symbol of a crown and sword-arm, his clan's motto, *Fac Et Spera*, "Do and Hope," emblazoned around the edge.

Shirt and boots on, sword once again belted around his waist, he collected his satchel, flipped open the leather flap then nabbed the remainder of his clothes from the trunk under the window and folded them inside. He crossed to the side table, his gut gnawing at him as he filled the basin with water from the jug and splashed his face. Even being only a few doors away from her was pure torture when all he wished to do was hold her in his arms and never let her go.

A knock sounded. "It's Tavish."

"Come in."

His brother strode inside with the padded cotun he'd worn earlier during training slung over one shoulder. Tavish closed the door after himself, a determined look on his face, one that likely matched his own. "Kirk has welcomed the MacDonalds into the keep. Donnan and his men are partaking of the midday meal in the great hall. Word is Donnan's here to stay until he and Layla have spoken vows at the end of the week. How'd your conversation with her go?"

"Very well, although she can't complete the bond with me until she's no longer betrothed to him. The guilt would consume her otherwise. I've told her I'll be the one who speaks to Donnan, which will need to be sooner rather than later." Bar of soap in hand, he lathered it then slapped the suds on his jaw. He unsheathed his wrist dagger and set to work shaving in front of the looking glass propped against the wall behind the basin.

"You're going to have a battle on your hands seeing to her release, but I'll be right by your side as you do." Tavish leaned his leather-clad backside on the stone windowsill, the forested hills rising high in the distance beyond the glass.

"I'm prepared for whatever battle it takes." In a firm line, he ran his blade from his ear to his chin, right side first then his left. "Is Julia available to sit with Layla in her chamber while I speak to Donnan? I don't want my mate anywhere near him."

"Julia's visiting kin at the fae village." Tavish tapped his head. "I can ask her to return. She rode out so she can be back within twenty minutes or so."

"Definitely ask her to come. You and I will wait with Layla until she arrives." He swiped his blade down his neck and in the small space between his nose and lips then once done, splashed the remaining suds away and dabbed his jaw dry with a drying cloth. With his dagger sheathed, he slung his bag over his shoulder and opened the door. He'd already been away from her for far too long, itched badly to return.

Down the corridor, he strode with Tavish at his side then outside Layla's door, he knocked and waited.

No answer.

"Layla?" He opened her door and the fresh breeze blew in through the open window and ruffled the thick burgundy curtains over her canopied bed. No Layla, not even a trace of her intoxicating wild cherry scent. "I told her to stay here."

"I didn't see her downstairs, or pass her on my way upstairs, so she can't have been gone from her chamber for too long." Tavish pulled his padded cotun on, palmed the hilt of his side-belted sword. "Gregor said she's always been fiercely independent, and certainly not very good at following orders whenever he issued them."

"Independence I like, except not right now." He hauled his

war coat from his bag, donned it then left his belongings on top of her wooden trunk before bounding downstairs to the great hall, Tavish one step behind him. He'd never allow her to talk to Donnan on her own. Not on his life.

The massive vaulted room held a sweeping crown of rafters rising to an impressive height. Tapestries of hunting and landscape scenes hung with pride around the vast room filled with a boisterous and hungry crowd. He searched the hall teeming with warriors wearing both MacDonald and Matheson plaids, but couldn't catch a glimpse of the one woman he needed to find. "I don't see her. Do you, Tavish?"

"I've got nothing, and worse, I don't see Donnan MacDonald either. The man's over six feet and wearing a great plaid, claymore sheathed in a baldric over his back. Dark brown hair that sits halfway down his back with war braids on each side, plus a scar cutting through his right eyebrow."

"Damn it." He couldn't see anyone of that description about either. He weaved around the perimeter of the hall, in and amongst the mingling warriors. Trestle tables overflowed with platters of bread, meats and cheeses, and other savory dishes. A serving girl with an apron tied around her waist approached with a tray of tankards in hand and he caught her elbow. "I'm looking for Layla, Effie. Have you seen her?"

"Aye, she left to take a walk with her betrothed." The lass motioned toward the front door. "If you hurry, you'll catch her."

He'd do more than catch her. Once he found his mate, he'd tie her to his very side, in every possible way. Completing the bond with her had now become imperative. No more could he wait.

* * * *

Layla climbed the trail leading up into the hills along the same pine-needle covered pathway she'd not long traversed down this morning with Tor, only this time she walked with Donnan at her back. Aye, allowing Tor to speak to Donnan wasn't a possibility, not when she'd been the one to accept the betrothal and since she'd gotten herself into this mess, she would be the one to get herself out of it, no matter what Tor wished or said.

"We seem to be going for quite the jaunt." Donnan stepped in beside her as the trail widened and came out at the stream that forked in two different directions. Along the waterway to the west lay the tip of their Matheson land which overlooked the ocean and the Isle of Skye across the sea, while to the east the stream ran through the forest and fields then joined a fast-flowing river which veered off toward the inner channel of Loch Alsh.

"This coming conversation is one I wish to keep between the two of us. I hope you dinnae mind."

"No' at all."

"Then wait right here for just a moment. Go no farther, please." She walked along the damp, mossy river bank a dozen steps then lifted her skirts and stepped into the stream. Should Tor follow her, then hopefully he'd be led in the opposite direction to where she was truly headed. Water splashed her ankles and calves as she back-tracked within the pebbly stream to Donnan's side. "Now, step in with me."

"Lass, do you mind telling me exactly where we're going?" With his great plaid secured over his broad chest with a silver pin and belted low at his waist with a leather girdle, Donnan appeared every inch the great warrior he was. "You're clearly wishing to evade someone. 'Tis impossible no' to notice."

"I promise to tell you soon." She would, once she'd gotten them a safer distance away and she had plenty of time to speak with him. Aye, her mate could track with his bear's senses, and far better than any other warrior could. "I'm going to levitate us both, Donnan. Are you ready?"

"Of course. This will be interesting."

With only a thought from her mind and a flick of her

fingers, she lifted them both up and sent them gliding downstream a foot or two above the water's rippling surface.

"Your fae skill is incredibly strong." Donnan eyed his feet, his war braids plaited at each side of his brown head blowing over his shoulders in the wind. "How fast can you move us like this?"

"Around the speed of a horse at full gallop."

"Marvelous."

"'Tis also rather helpful, particularly in moments like these." She continued on, breezing them through the forest until it gave way to the rolling moors, the craggy hills rising higher on their right and the inner channel of Loch Alsh sitting just beyond the wide open field to their left. She left the stream behind and whizzed across the land bobbing with heather and awash with wildflowers. Her heart lifted at being so at one with nature, although her soul heaved at the distance she'd now instilled between her and Tor. He'd never be able to track her, not now. Goodness. He would be furious that she'd left the castle without him, but her decision to do so was a wise one and she was safe in Donnan's hands. Along with Father, she'd spent a good fortnight on the Isle of Skye at Dunscaith Castle with Donnan and his clan during the time leading up to their betrothal agreement being formalized.

"'Tis almost as if I have wings and can soar like a bird." Donnan lifted his face to the sky and breathed deep before glancing at her. "I believe we're getting close to your warrior encampment, where the recent battle with Colin MacKenzie took place. Is that correct?"

"Aye, you're right. The encampment is very close. I'll take you there if you wish." He nodded his agreement and she left the field behind, skimmed around the edge of the woods and breezed alongside the sandy shoreline of the loch. Time passed and the sun slowly lowered, its golden rays rippling across the jewel blues of the water while up ahead, the bay curved and tents dotted the edge of the forest running alongside their mountainous land border between them and clan MacKenzie, their cruelest and bitterest enemy. She gently settled them both back down on the beach, a short walk from the camp. "We'll walk from here so we might have that opportunity to speak."

"I can see you'll be a treasure to have at my side." Donnan offered her his arm and she slipped her hand through the crook at his elbow. As they wandered along the shoreline, he cleared his throat. "The knowledge of what you and your father can do, will always remain a secret, one my father has kept between him and my clansmen, and one I too shall keep with my men. Is that what you wished to speak to me about?"

"I'm aware you and your father have kept the secret of my father's ability to yourselves, and mine too since learning of it. 'Tis of another matter altogether that I wish to speak to you about."

"Then tell me." His two-handed claymore bobbed in a baldric across his back, the burnished hilt glinting in the waning light. "You can speak freely with me. Never fear that you cannae."

"My father waited three years after I came of age afore he signed the binding betrothal agreement, his desire to ensure I wasnae soul bound to another, the reason why." She halted on the beach, let go of him and clasped her hands before her, straightened her shoulders and her never-ending resolve.

"Aye, and glad I am that you're no' soul bound to another as many of your fae kind are." He stopped, towering a good foot over her as he eyed her.

"Ah, well, things have now changed." She rocked from foot to foot. "My mate, the one my soul is bound to, has now tracked me down and made it very clear he willnae allow me to wed another. I'm so sorry, Donnan, but I cannae marry you, no' when my mate holds the other half of my soul and I too wish to be with him."

His gaze narrowed then he snorted and shook his head. "Our betrothal," he issued between clenched teeth, "cannae be broken. We are already as good as wed and should I lie with you right now, right here on this beach and consummate our agreement, then none would ever gainsay my decision to do so. You would be my wife in truth."

"Yet should I honor our betrothal agreement and speak vows with you, I would still forever long for him. Is that what you want? A wife who yearns for another?" She had to make him see reason.

"Give me his name and I'll ensure you cannae yearn for him for long." He ran one finger along the length of his jeweled wrist dagger. "I can dispense with him, quickly and assuredly. My sons will hold fae blood. 'Tis my duty to my clan to ensure it and your duty to your clan to honor our agreement. Tell me the man's name and I'll deal with the wretch."

"Nay, you must accept my decision."

"Speak his name, Layla. I demand that you do." He thumped his fisted hands against his chest then let out a mighty roar. The thundering rumble echoed along the loch and sent birds nesting in the long grasses squawking and scattering into the sky. "I will have his head, lass, and you willnae stop me."

* * * *

Tor knelt within the woods and touched the lighter footstep along the stream's embankment belonging to Layla and the heavier print of Donnan MacDonald's. He and Tavish had already followed the stream to the end of their Matheson land which overlooked the ocean and the Isle of Skye, but they hadn't as yet found any further signs of either Layla or Donnan's tracks reemerging along the entire route. Agitated, he rose to his feet. "She's clearly used her skill to get away from me."

"We'll track her down. It's impossible for anyone to fully hide from a bear." Tavish bounded back across the stream in his black pants and tunic then motioned toward the east where the warrior encampment lay at the end of the inner channel of Loch Alsh. "At least we've only one more direction to search."

"Keep a lookout for any trace of movement within the stones along the river base as well."

"Will do."

Nose to the air, Tor strode along the side of the stream searching for any lingering scent of his mate while his brother combed the other side. They tramped a good mile before they left the forest behind and followed the stream as it weaved across the rolling moors. It was as if his mate hadn't passed in this direction either, except his gut told him she had. He scanned the horizon, from the craggy hills rising higher on their right to the inner channel of Loch Alsh sitting just beyond the moors to their left. She couldn't hide from him forever. He'd never allow it. "Once I find her," he said through gritted teeth to his brother, "it'll be a hell of a long time before I ever allow her out of my sight again."

Never had he felt so lost or so furious. If any harm had come to her because he'd misjudged the strength of her fierce nature and her desperate need to protect him, then he'd never survive it. She was his to care for, his to keep safe from any and all harm.

Marching on, he left the stream behind and gave his bear his head as he stormed across the rolling fields of heather swaying with an array of wildflowers. "We'll work in a crisscross pattern and head toward the loch," he called to Tavish. "We'll be able to call on the aid of the warriors from the encampment if we don't find her before we reach the camp."

"Understood." Tavish picked up his pace, searching the fields with determination, just as he did. They crossed paths as they weaved back and forth across the terrain then his brother lowered to his haunches in the thick grass next to some low brush. "Tor, I've found something."

He jogged across and knelt next to his brother. Snagged

within the scrub, a long strand of curly blond hair fluttered in the breeze. He plucked the length of hair free, brought it to his nose and dragged in his mate's glorious, wild cherry scent. "At least we now know for certain she came through—"

"Tell me his name!" The thunderous roar echoed from up ahead along the shoreline.

"There they are." Tavish jabbed a finger and Tor found the outline of two people on the beach before the glittering water, one towering menacingly over the other.

He sprinted across the moors, his heartbeat a raging mess. Over the sand dunes, he bounded then with a fierce battle cry and his head down, he rammed into Donnan MacDonald and sent them both skittering across the sand.

Chapter 5

Layla screamed as Tor roared and crashed into Donnan. The two men went flying, sprayed sand as they rolled across the beach then pulled apart and heaved to their feet. Tor swung his sword from his side scabbard and Donnan whipped his claymore from the baldric across his back.

The two came together with a mighty crash of their great blades.

Steel sparked, the brutal force of their strike sending both of them lurching back a step under the jarring impact. "There is naught I like more than an eager opponent," Donnan snarled.

"I'm beyond eager." Tor thrust his sword high and blocked Donnan's next swift blow.

"I take it you're the man my betrothed is soul bound to?" Donnan's eyes blazed with hatred, a fierce and fiery look that spoke of intended retribution.

"Aye, the name's Tor Matheson." Tor shoved against him. "Layla is my mate and only mine." He struck hard and fast, landing several hard blows as he fought to push Donnan farther from her and toward the waves lapping into shore.

"You both have to cease this fighting." She hurried forward but Tavish swept her up from behind and carried her backward to safety. "Let me go, Tavish."

"This is Tor's fight, not yours," Tavish rasped in her ear as he set her down on her feet, gripped her arms from behind. "Let him deal with Donnan. Trust him. My brother won't fail you."

"I won't have my kinsmen go to war against clan MacDonald because of me." She thrashed against Tavish. "Tor, please, halt this madness."

Donnan swung and Tor met the staggering blow, although it knocked him to his knees, his blade and Donnan's crossing a mere inch from his nose. Tor's arms shook as he gripped his great sword and heaved back to his feet.

"Keep Layla with you and out of this fight," Tor yelled at Tavish.

"I'll keep her safe."

Tor cast her a look. "We'll be talking, the moment this battle is done."

"Just keep your eyes on the fight."

"Aye, you should never lose sight of your opponent." Donnan shot forward and landed a vicious blow on Tor's left.

Tor shuddered under the impact and fought back. She wanted to use her skill to tear them both apart, but they moved so brutally fast she'd likely do more harm than good if she tried to separate them.

"Layla will be my wife, and afore this day is out. I'll ensure it." Donnan swung, each of his strikes slamming home with deadlier intent.

"Like hell she will." Tor met each of Donnan's blows, one after the other. Their weapons clashed, the heavy peal of steel on steel ringing fiercely in her ears. Over and over, they came at each other, Donnan landing several solid blows before Tor did the same with Donnan.

"You clearly favor your right side, Matheson." Donnan twirled and attacked on Tor's left, each hit stronger than the last.

"I favor no side." Tor switched sword hands and fought on.

Sweat beaded his brow as he gained back ground and pushed Donnan back. "What of you?"

"I favor a win, however that may be achieved, which means I will have your head. No one steals my betrothed away from me and lives to speak of it." Donnan swung his claymore and Tor defended then struck himself. They were so evenly matched, in power, height, and skill, neither man prepared to relinquish any hold over the other.

A horn trumpeted from the direction of the encampment and two heavily armed warriors galloped down the beach toward them, their Matheson plaids flapping about their legs. Gerald rode at the head, one of their garrison's captains and her father's closest confidant.

"Gerald!" she yelled and waved. "Please, you have to stop this fight."

Gerald bounded from his war horse and circled the battling men. "What's the meaning of this, Tor?"

"Don't come any closer." Tor rocked on his heels and blocked Donnan's next fierce strike then dropped low, rolled clear and came up behind him. He swung and Donnan barely caught the staggering blow. Donnan fell to his knees and Tor slid his sword right up against Donnan's throat. "Concede to your defeat," he barked. "Layla is my mate, the woman I intend to wed."

"You'll never wed her while she's betrothed to me." Donnan's arms shook as he tried to keep Tor's blade from slicing into him.

"I want your word, spoken right now before these witnesses, that you repudiate your betrothal." Tor pushed his blade down firmer, right into Donnan's skin. A drop of blood welled. "I will never allow you near my chosen one again. Do you hear me, MacDonald?"

Donnan glared, his chest rising and falling as he heaved in a breath. Tor needed to shove only a little harder and his blade would slice right through Donnan's throat. With a venomous glare, Donnan snapped out, "I repudiate my betrothal." He shot her a fierce look. "You are free to wed your warrior. If. You. Dare."

Damn it. Now she'd gone and ensured their greatest ally had become their greatest enemy. She couldn't have botched her talk up with Donnan more than she had. Aye, she'd set both clans against each other and she couldn't see any possible way to make amends.

"Lower your weapon." Tor's blade scraped Donnan's flesh and another drop of blood oozed out.

"I concede." Donnan slowly lowered his blade then dropped it.

"Gerald." Tor gritted his teeth as he grasped Donnan's weapon and lobbed it to the man. "See our visitor off our land and ensure he never returns. I want you to report back to me once that has happened."

"Of course." Gerald gestured to the other Matheson warrior who'd rode with him from the encampment to dismount then offered the spare horse to Donnan who grumbled as he mounted the black steed.

Layla held her breath as Donnan shoved his knees into his horse's flanks and galloped over the sand dunes and across the moors with Gerald riding at his side. She remained right where she stood until the two riders become naught more than a mere dot on the horizon.

Tor caught her arm, turned her to face him. "We'll stay at the encampment until Gerald returns with word that Donnan and his men have sailed back to Skye. I don't want you anywhere near the keep until I'm assured he's gone."

"I am so mad at you right now. You put your life on the line for mine and you shouldnae have." Never had fear and fury clashed within her so fiercely. Father and her entire clan would soon know exactly what had happened and of how she'd destroyed their longstanding relationship with their allied clan. Tor hadn't helped in making certain all had gone well either, his usually level head having flown right out the window from the moment he'd arrived and taken Donnan to the ground. So much for having a civil conversation about ending her betrothal with the man she'd been set to wed. Her frustration doubled, her fear for Tor now tripling after hearing Donnan's threat about ending her mate's life and having his head. This was all her fault. Tor could have been so easily killed this day because of her.

Madder at herself than Tor, she stormed along the curve of the bay toward the encampment, the setting sun dropping below the horizon and sending a last flare of red spearing through the darkening sky.

She passed a large group of shirtless warriors battling hard on the grassy shoreline, while near a small island in the middle of the bay, one holding a copse of trees and a wooden shack, a good thirty men swam in then jogged out of the water and swapped out with the battling warriors.

"I'll catch up with you two later. I'd like to join in with the training before the evening meal." Tavish left them, headed toward the makeshift corral of beams hammered between the trees, stripped off his shirt and weapons then bounded into the loch.

"Layla, wait up."

"Leave me be, Tor. I'm in no mood to talk right now." She brushed him off as she hurried past the central fire and the camp cook in her brown woolen kirtle. The elderly woman stirred stew in a blackened pot bubbling over the sizzling flames. "Which is the ladies' tent?" she asked the cook. "I would like to rest."

"'Tis the one right at the end and 'tis all yours if you wish it." The cook wiped one hand on her apron as she tipped her head in the direction Layla needed to go. "Cherub used it last, but she remains at the castle now."

"Thank you." She stalked to the tent near the forest's edge

and past another group of warriors who aimed their arrows at a white ribbon tied around a wide trunk a hundred feet distant. Each warrior stepped forward to take his turn with the bow. With impressive accuracy, arrow after arrow thunked into the thin strip of silk.

"We need to talk, Layla, and it can't wait." Tor swept past her, lifted the tent flap and motioned for her to go in. "I won't permit you to brush me off."

"I'm too mad right now to talk to anyone. 'Tis best if you allow me some time to calm down." She ducked inside and paced the tent, from canvas wall to wall, Tor remaining solidly in the center, hands planted on his hips as he eyed her.

"You should never have snuck away from the keep. You made damn certain you would be nearly impossible to find, and that's totally unacceptable to me." With a low growl, he shrugged his war coat off and tossed it on top of the wooden crate next to a lamp. "You're my mate, mine to protect and care for."

"I snuck away for a very good reason."

"Explain your reasoning to me." He struck flint with his dagger and lit the lamp, its flame flickering within the darkening tent and casting its soft glow over the canvas walls.

"To speak to Donnan, to break the betrothal I agreed to. So too I would have had the conversation under control if you had no' have stormed in."

"Like hell you would have." He caught her around the waist as she made her next pass and dragged her up against his heaving chest. "I don't even want to think about the fact that Donnan could have forced a consummation of your betrothal vows and made you his wife in truth this very day. No one would have gainsaid his decision with the signed agreement in place if he'd done so. I could have lost you, forever."

"I would never have allowed Donnan to touch me, or to sway me to his way of thinking. I fully intended to explain things to him, to ensure he understood my position and to have him release me from our agreement."

"You're my mate, and I would give my life to ensure your protection."

"Donnan may have repudiated our betrothal, but only under duress. He will return, seek retribution, make his demands known. 'Tis just a matter of time."

"Let him. Next time I'll not issue a reprieve as I did this day." He walked her backward until the backs of her knees hit the corner pile of brown fur pelts and she toppled back onto them. Swiftly, he sank down on top of her, tipped her head to the side and bared her neck. He licked her flesh, right over his mark then looked deep into her eyes. "We need to complete the bond. Once we do, we'll have a merged link of the mind, one that is inherent in my shifter blood. We'll be able to speak to each other at will along a pathway known only to us, mind to mind, and that connection will ensure I can always remain in touch with you. Only then will both me and my bear ever be at peace."

"The last thing I wish for is such a merged link." A complete lie. She would adore it, not that she was telling him that right now. Mayhap not ever.

"I never want you to leave my side again." He dipped his head once more, razzed his teeth over the mark, and damn it, she shivered with need.

"Dinnae you dare bite me, Tor Matheson."

"I won't apologize for coming to your rescue, and I will be biting you." His low rumble vibrated against her heaving chest, his gaze imploring. "Say aye, my challenging mate. I need your permission before I do."

"Nay, and we are in the middle of an argument if you have no' noticed."

"You're so beautiful when you get mad. I haven't told you that yet, but I should have." He grinned, actually grinned and she wanted to slap him. Clearly her mate had no self-preservation.

"Release me." She pushed against his rock hard chest, except he moved not an inch.

"Layla, when you went missing"—his tone gentled, his golden gaze heating as he rubbed the tip of his nose against hers—"I realized something very important, that there isn't a chance I can ever live without you. I nearly went insane when I couldn't find you. Let me bite you. You must allow it."

"You are far too forceful for my liking."

"And kiss you. You must allow me a kiss as well." He slid one hand around the back of her head and seized her hip with the other. Rubbing his body against hers, he embedded his deliciously earthly fresh scent into her. "My bear is rampaging inside me. I'll have to shift soon, and the last thing I want to do is leave you like this, when both of us have been fighting. Grant me a kiss, please."

She truly shouldn't allow him to have his way like this, only the need lacing his tone sent that thought flittering from her head. She touched her lips to his, their kiss brief and almost over before it had even begun, but a kiss all the same. "Now leave."

"Huh." He snorted under his breath. "I clearly should have stipulated how long that kiss should have been, but still I thank you for it all the same." He groaned then rolled off her onto his back on the pelts, his gaze on the tented ceiling above. He squeezed his eyes shut then opened them again and slowly sat up. He removed his weapons, shucked his boots and hauled his loose-sleeved black tunic over his head before standing in his faded brown rawhide pants. "Turn around if you wish. I need to fully disrobe."

"How long will you be gone?" She lifted the circlet headband of silk flowers from her hair and set it on top of the crate next to his war coat, kicked off her slippers and unknotted the tasseled blue ties of her leather girdle then tossed the belt on top of her belongings. "Will you be back this eve, or sleeping elsewhere?"

"I'll sleep here. You can take one side of the tent and I'll take the other, if that's what you desire."

"I certainly do." She fidgeted with the white lace edging her gown's long sleeves, not wanting him to leave at all, or for him to sleep so far away from her. This bond was completely impossible, her need for him roaring to full force now he was so close to leaving her. She didn't want him to shift, or go. Argh, so frustrating.

"Then that is what it shall be." He hauled a couple of pelts off the pile and spread them on the other side of the tent then loosened the ties of his pants at his waist. "Last chance to turn around."

Her throat clogged and she tried to push away the fear rising within her. Fighting with him felt so very wrong and instinct took over. She needed to keep him here with her, apologize in some way. Her temper had risen fast, but also fallen just as swiftly away. With no more thought, she shoved her sleeves down her arms and shimmied the royal blue velvet down over her hips until it fell in a soft swish to the floor. In her shift, she scooped up her gown and hung it on the hook protruding from the center pole then stepped in front of him. "Disrobe as you wish."

Tor watched her, his gaze moving over her body then he nodded, pushed his pants down and kicked them off. In the flickering light from the lamp, every inch of his heavily muscled body gleamed, from his wide chest and trim hips to his manhood lengthening and rising from a thatch of dark curls at the apex of his groin.

"My turn." No turning back. No more would they fight. Life was too short for arguments. She gripped her shift's hem, lifted the cotton up and over her head then hooked it over top of her gown on the pole. Heat flushed her cheeks, but she wouldn't allow any further embarrassment to take her. He was her mate and he held the other half of her soul. He'd also battled Donnan and made him repudiate their betrothal. She couldn't deny she was now free to be with him. "I wish you an enjoyable romp in the woods," she murmured, her body on full display for him alone.

"Thank you," he whispered, his words ragged as he trailed a finger down her neck then gently, carefully, he scooped her breasts up and dipped his head. He licked one nipple and the hot rasp of his tongue across her sensitive flesh doubled the flurry of need pulsing through her.

She cupped the back of his head, scraped her nails lightly over his scalp. More need rushed through her and she guided his mouth to hers and kissed him, with all the longing she held deep within her heart. 'Twas time to set all her fears aside and trust only the man to whom she truly desired. Having his warm lips moving over hers and the hard length of his body pressed against her, fueled her need for even more.

With one thought from her mind, she lifted them both up and laid them down on the pelts, her underneath him and her mate on top, his hot shaft pressed firmly against her belly and every inch of him a delicious weight she wanted more of. "Grant me one more kiss afore you shift and leave," she breathed against his lips. "And I wish to stipulate that it be a long one."

"One long kiss coming up." He captured her mouth with his and kissed her, the heat of his body wrapped around hers making her cling to him for more.

Breasts pressed against the wicked heat of his chest, she stroked her thumb over the mark she'd given him on his neck. Her mouth watered with the desire to bite him again, to have him bite her in return and lay claim to her in every single way. She leaned in, sucked his skin deep into her mouth then bit down, hard and fast.

He lifted his head and roared, his bear so close to the surface. Fur rippled across his chest and down his arms, a soft padding of silk there one moment and gone the next.

"Shh." She giggled and clamped a hand over his mouth. "These canvas walls are thin."

A tap sounded on the wooden pole out front. "Is everything all right in there?"

"Aye, all is fine," she called back to one of her kinsmen. She giggled again then nipped along Tor's jaw and sucked on his ear. "Do you still need to shift?"

"Not if you're going to keep laving attention on me like this. I promise to keep my bear at bay."

"May I touch you?"

"Any part of me you wish. My body is yours, as is my heart and soul if you choose to accept me."

"I accept you, every single infuriating inch of you. I hope you can handle a fiercely strong woman." She caressed his shoulders and arms, so thick and strong then fluttered her fingers over the firm planes of his wide chest. His abs rippled, layer upon firm layer and she swished down the rigid center, along the delicious tease of dark hair narrowing down his belly and along his waist. With her skill, she lifted him up a touch until he floated an inch or two above her. Sweet heaven. The head of his shaft had thickened further and now flushed a bright and delectable cherry color.

She needed all the kisses he could give her, every mark of claim and anything else he was willing to offer. She ran her thumb across his warm lips and a whole lot breathless, murmured, "'Tis time."

"Show me it's time." He caught her hands, pressed them high over her head and against the pelts she lay on. As her fingertips brushed the canvas wall behind her, she arched into his touch, spread her legs and lowered him back down on top of her.

She closed her eyes as a sizzle of sensation rippled through her then opened them again. Having his flesh against her flesh and naught else separating them made every inch of her crave him all the more. "Touch me wherever and however you please,

Tor. I need to feel your hands on me."

"I hold the same need but if you want me to stop at any time, then tell me." He licked her lower lip. "I'll understand."

"There's no stopping the completion of our bond."

"Then we'll take it slow. You'll tell me what you like, what you don't like, what you want more of, or what you don't want more of. I've no wish to hurt you, to take from you what you're not yet ready to give."

"I want to be with you, in every possible way." *Time is of the essence.* Nessa's prophetic warning rang in her ears. "Be mine."

"In order to complete the bond, we'll need to be skin on skin. Which means there'll be a chance you could conceive." He released her hands and shuffled down, his warm breath feathering across the flatness of her belly. He pressed his palm there, then dropped a gentle kiss on her skin. "Is that acceptable?"

"I dinnae fear having a babe, no' when I long for children." She sank her fingers into his shoulders and gasped as he licked around her belly button.

"I'd love nothing more than to give you a child, my child." He brushed his nose along the underside of her breasts, nipped in a circle around each mound then cupped them both and smoothed his thumbs over the peaking tips. "In the future, very few women die in childbirth since medically speaking, we're far more advanced. I'll never lose you as your father lost your mother."

"Promise?"

"I give you my word. I've waited so long to find you, and there isn't a chance I'll ever lose you, not now. I'll make certain of it." He sucked her nipple deep into his mouth then moved to the other and drew it between his lips. He played the tip to perfection and heat rippled through her. Her body undulated under his, all on its own accord and she couldn't halt her need or contain it.

"Layla, there's one more thing we need to speak of before we go any further." Gently, he caught her hand, brought it to his mouth and kissed her palm. His gaze heated, burning an even richer golden hue. "Marry me this night. Be my wife."

"You wish to wed me, now?" Her heartbeat raced.

"I do." He suctioned his mouth over her nipple again and she moaned as he devoured her, sucking and licking her.

"Aye," she gasped. Tears filled her eyes and slid down her cheeks as sheer happiness overflowed her. "I want you as my husband."

"We'll speak handfast vows since I've no intention of finding a clergyman at this time of the night, or leaving this tent for that matter. Bind yourself to me now, for the next year and a day and the moment I can get you before a priest, I will." He reached out, nabbed his pants from the floor, pulled her hair ribbon out and grinning, clasped her right hand with his right hand and wrapped the red silk around both their wrists.

"You are a very clever mate."

"And determined. I'll go first." He breathed deep, his gaze locked tight with hers. "Layla, I offer you my full protection, that of my body, my clan, my family, and all that I am. I give myself to you freely. Give yourself to me freely in return."

"I will."

"Thank you." He brought their joined hands to his mouth and kissed her knuckles. "I, Tor David Matheson, of Ivanson Castle, pledge my troth to Layla, of the House of Clan Matheson. With this handfast, I take her as my wife for the next year and a day, and as my soul bound mate for all time." He tightened his grip on her hand. "Be mine, in every single way."

With her fingers twined with his, she nodded. There could be no other way. He had stolen her heart and would hold it for the rest of their lives. "I, Layla, of the House of Clan Matheson, pledge my troth to Tor David Matheson. With this handfast, I take him as my husband for the next year and a day, and as my soul bound mate for all time." She touched the silk bound around their wrists and smiled. "Glad I am that you are mine."

"Now we seal the vows with a kiss, or I should say, many kisses." He kissed the tips of her breasts, making them all wet and shiny before he fondled the hard nubs and kissed his way up and along her neck.

She couldn't halt her hips from pushing against his. He'd awakened her body, opened her heart and soul and taken full and complete possession of every single inch of her. She craved his touch. Her warrior shifter was beyond beautiful, and this bond which tied them together, was one she would never relinquish. Every hard and defined inch of him was now hers for the taking.

Needing to touch him, she released the ribbon and it fluttered to the fur. She tickled her fingers down his sides and swept one hand around his thick shaft. It throbbed hot and heavy in her hand.

"Layla." He groaned into her neck, brushed his hand over her entrance, his intimate touch a sweet caress she wanted more of. Then he drove one finger inside her and stroked deep, curling his finger into a spot that had her straining for more. "Does this feel all right?"

"There is naught you cannae do that I willnae love. I'm certain of it. Keep touching me."

"I will…my wife." Looking into her eyes, he lowered his mouth to hers and kissed her, so deeply and so poignantly. Her heart tripped over itself as she worked him in long pulls below and he moved his finger inside her to the same instinctual rhythm. Then he lifted his head with a low moan. "I'm going to come if you keep touching me like that. I have very little willpower right now."

"There is no need for willpower around me." She swiped her thumb over the essence leaking from the tip of his shaft then brought her thumb to her mouth and tentatively licked it. Mmm, he tasted divine, salty and strong, and she wanted to taste more of him. "Tor, I have a wee confession to make. Once, a few months past when I was unable to sleep, I snuck outside and as I passed the stables, I caught the sounds of grunting and other strange noises coming from within. My curiosity got the better of me and I crept inside and halted within the shadows. A warrior stood with his back pressed to the planked wall, his eyes closed in rapture as a serving lass knelt in the soft hay afore him. His trews lay in a puddle at his feet and the lass dipped her head and the man groaned and grasped her face as she took his shaft into her mouth. I should have backed away and left them to their loving, but in all honesty, I couldnae move. I was struck by the raw beauty of the moment. The warrior seemed helpless, as if the lass on her knees commanded him and soon after, he let out a boisterous shout and toppled the lass onto the hay. I would like to pleasure you as the lass pleasured her warrior, with my mouth on you below."

"So, it seems I've wed a sneaky lass?"

"Aye, you have." Gently, she swirled her thumb over the head of his cock and another drop beaded on the tip.

"If you do that again and taste me like you just did, I'll likely lose it." He stretched out over her and rumbled as fur shimmered over his chest then retracted. "My bear is in heaven right now and so am I. I need a taste of you first, and it can't wait another moment." He raised up, knelt between her legs, his balls drawing firmer and higher, his shaft thickening and lengthening even further. Licking his lips, he spread her legs wider and gazed at her below. "So beautiful."

"You mean to taste me there?" She hadn't seen the warrior do that to the lass. The man had plunged his cock between her nether lips and taken her hard and fast once the lass no longer had her mouth around him.

"Absolutely. Tasting each other goes both ways, and honestly, I wanted to do this earlier when I had you in your chamber. You came so quickly though, that you didn't give me a chance to do so."

"Will I like it?" A myriad of emotions tumbled through her at his words, from fierce desire to complete and utter need. She'd never wished for a soul bound mate, but now she couldn't imagine living her life without the man who held her to him in every way. She opened her heart wider, wanted only to draw him ever deeper inside and meld their lives together, in all ways.

"I intend for you to love it. One day I'll explain movies to you and what I too might have found interesting while watching them in my time." With her legs raised, he hooked them over his shoulders until her bottom lifted off the bed and she lay fully exposed to him. His silky black hair swept over her skin as he lowered his head between her open thighs and spread her folds.

"One moment." Goodness. The sight of his head between her legs and his tongue darting out sent her heart slamming against her ribs. She sank her fingers into his hair and held onto him.

"You're so pink and lush, my love, beyond enticing and completely all mine."

Never had a man been so enraptured by her. "I'm ready."

"I'm beyond ready." He licked her then moaned and dived in deeper. His tongue probed all around, flicked deep then swiped over her nub. She gasped and arched deeper into his touch. 'Twas all too much, yet also not nearly enough.

Every inch of her body tingled and she clutched his head and held him possessively to her as a firestorm of need radiated out from where he touched. He gripped her hips, his claws extending then retracting as his mouth moved like a hot brand over her nub. He sucked, hard, built her pleasure to a soaring level. "Tor." She thrashed underneath him. "Please, come inside me. I dinnae wish to reach this peak without you."

"I'm coming." He lifted his head, his gaze on hers as he rose over top of her. With one hand on his shaft, he rubbed the head along her sensitized folds, coating himself in her wetness below before he pressed the tip to her channel and gazed into her eyes.

She cupped his cheeks and drew him closer to her. "Do it."

"I can't take the pain of our joining away, but I'll make it pass as quickly as I can."

"I can handle the pain, particularly when all I want is this joining." Something battered against her mind and she wrapped her legs around his waist as he nudged his cock against her barrier. "Be mine, Tor, always mine."

"Always, from this moment forth." His mind shoved against the barrier still locked in place between their minds and he grimaced, a flare of anguish crossing his face. Her big bear had such a tender heart, truly didn't wish to cause her even a moment of pain.

Grasping his buttocks and with a mental push from her mind, she sent him plunging inside her and as he tore through her barrier, his mind tunneled deep inside hers as he created the private pathway that would only ever be theirs. Joined together, both in body and mind, she was laid completely bare to him and 'twas all she desired. No more secrets. Her thoughts would be there for him to read, and his thoughts hers for the taking. Such a stunning connection. She seized the link, locked it into place within her mind and whispered into his, "*My husband, my lover, my fierce steward.*"

"*It feels incredible to have you in my mind and for me to be in yours.*" Slowly, he lifted up, drew himself out then moaned and pushed all the way back in again until his balls slid sensuously against the inside of her thighs.

Rocking underneath him, her heart and body his for the taking, she moaned right along with him. "*I love how you feel inside of me.*"

"*I'm sure I love it more. How's the pain?*"

"*It wasnae so bad. All I feel now is very full, and also a great deal of desire for you to keep moving.*" She clung to him, her arms wound tightly around his neck and her ankles crossed over his backside.

"*I will, but keep your mind open to mine so I can feel what brings you pleasure and what might not.*" He pulled out and pushed back in, going deeper with each long penetrating drive. Thrusting, he quickened his pace, his mouth on her neck as he sucked at her skin.

"*Are you going to bite me?*" She couldn't wait for him to.

"*Aye, the same time you're going to bite me.*" He palmed the back of her head, brought her mouth to his neck as he pounded into her.

She rocked with him and grazed her teeth back and forth over his fiercely beating pulse. Sensations stormed to full and fiery life within her, until she could no longer hold her need back. She marked him, as swiftly and possessively as any woman would in claiming her mate. Her warrior. Her bear. Her husband.

"*Do that again,*" he demanded as he plunged into her, over and over, his pace wildly frantic.

Heartbeat thumping against his, she bucked and bit down, marking him a second time. He roared his pleasure then sank his teeth into her and sent every one of her last thoughts careening. She cried out his name, his masterful claiming such pure pleasure and passion all rolled into one, a joining she'd crave for the rest of her life. Of that she had no doubt.

"*You feel so good coming around me.*" He caressed her nub with one finger and her channel squeezed his cock ruthlessly as she dragged him even deeper inside her. His seed pulsed from him, coating her inside and her heart soared right along with her soul as they connected on a level far beyond this place and time.

She nuzzled his neck, lapped at his skin. She wanted him, just like this, with him never leaving her side. Living without him wasn't an option and if he ever perished, then so would she.

Their mated bond was a slice of heaven and now she knew how beautiful it was to hold him deep inside her, she'd never give him up. To the depths of her being, she was his, for now and for all time.

* * * *

A red haze of lust consumed Tor's mind and a powerful surge of need still clamored within him. Even though he'd just claimed his woman in every possible way, he moved his mouth to the other side of her neck and with her pulse hammering out of time under his tongue, he bit down and marked her again.

Thrusting balls-deep, his essence continued to stream from him and her heavenly channel rippled over and over, squeezing him as she rode the sizzling waves of her orgasm right along with him.

"I need more," she murmured, her body locked tight around his, her mind moving through and saturating him deep within. He clutched onto her, shared his own need and reveled as she grinned and stretched out underneath him, her desire for more just as strong as his was. Only first, he needed to ensure all was well with her.

Carefully, he eased his rocking and brought them slowly back down as tenderly as he could. On his elbows, he lifted up a touch so he wasn't pressing his entire weight down on her. Her beautiful breasts bobbed in front of him and he groaned at the temptation he'd never get enough of. Her creamy skin and the slender column of her neck, lured him in as nothing else could. He licked each of the marks he'd stamped across her flesh, around her neck and over her breasts. His bear purred and rolled around with delight inside him. Happy bear. Happy man.

"I love having your mouth on me, Tor."

"Where exactly?"

"Everywhere."

"You taste incredible, like the sweetest honey and my bear and I are already addicted to the taste." Still wedged deep inside her, his cock stirred back to full and needy life once more. Hell, he wanted to take her all over again, but first he'd take care of her. Even though it pained him to leave her body, he slid out.

"Where are you going?" She rubbed against the fur pelt she lay on, her back arching. She was an ethereal vision, all sensuous curves and a feast unlike any he'd ever beheld.

"To tend to you first." A streak of blood lay smeared along her inner thigh. She'd given him her innocence, just as he'd given her his, and his bear rumbled with pleasure. "There's blood and I need to make sure all is well. Wait right here. I'll grab some water and tend to you."

"I dinnae want you to go."

"There's a barrel of water just outside. I'll be but a moment." He hooked one of the furs around his waist, grabbed his empty skin and snuck outside. Stars glittered within the heavenly blanket of black sweeping the sky and the moon shone bright. All within the camp had gone quiet, the fire blazing in the center now surrounded by warriors who'd bedded down around its warmth. They'd missed the evening meal, not that he hungered for anything more than another taste of his handfast wife right now. As moonlight glittered over the stillness of the loch and the slight rustle of nighttime creatures moving within the forest resounded toward him, he dipped the skin in the barrel at the forest's edge, filled it and plugged the cork. He loosened the fur at his waist, splashed a handful of water over his cock then refastened the fur and snuck back inside the tent.

Layla smiled wickedly, moved onto her hands and knees on the fur. She crawled toward him, her blond locks sliding forward and swaying in front of her full breasts. As she reached the end of their makeshift bed, she rose up onto her knees and crooked a finger at him. "Come here."

"Have a drink first." He passed her the skin and she took a sip while he tossed the fur from around his waist aside, swiped a cloth from a pile on the crate in one corner and dropped to his knees before her.

"Here you go." She passed him the skin back and he tipped her back onto the pelts, gently eased her legs apart and kneeling between them, wet the cloth with water from his pouch and wiped the blood away. "Do you hurt here?"

"A little." Her soulful brown gaze softened. "But in a wonderful way. I've finally found what I've been missing from my life. You."

"As I've now found you." He'd never felt more complete, as if the missing piece of his soul was back and now held safely within her hands. Carefully, he cleaned her, until every trace of their joining was gone then he plugged the skin and tossed it aside. He curled his hands around her hips, pressed a soft kiss to her mound and nuzzled the thatch of golden curls covering her entrance before touching his tongue to her clit.

She gasped, caught his face in her hands and giggled as she tugged him up. "Everything feels so sensitive."

"Do you need me to wait before I touch you there again?"

"Aye, but apparently you dinnae need any such wait. You appear ripe for my touch." Her gaze moved over his heavy erection and with a devious lift to her brow, she lifted his body up with her skill and laid him down on his back on the fur. She crawled in between his legs, her breasts swaying softly either side of his balls as she leaned in.

With the lightest of touches, she curled one hand around his shaft then dipped her head and licked him from root to tip.

Hell, her touch was exquisite.

"Do you like this?"

"I love having your mouth on me. Touch me as you wish, however you wish. My body is yours, just as yours is mine." He craved her touch, to the depths of his soul.

"I caught that thought." She grinned as she peered at him through her long, sooty lashes, her mind moving swiftly through his. Head dipped again, she moved her lips over him and took him deep as she fondled his balls in the palm of her hand.

Pleasure slammed into him, made him clench his butt and hold on for the ride of his life.

"Mmm, you taste delicious." Desire flared in her eyes as she gazed at him, her head bobbing up and down as she worked his cock with her beautiful mouth.

"I intend to repay this favor the moment I can." He cradled her head in his hands, his cock hardening impossibly further as she found a rhythm that would soon send him soaring from his body. A heat unlike any he'd ever felt sizzled at the base of his spine and ricocheted around and blazed like fire in his groin. Heat curled his toes, had his claws slicing out and his bear roaring to the surface. He barely held his beast back. No more. He couldn't take another moment of this exquisite torture.

"*A little longer, please,*" she whispered in his mind and almost undid him. For her, he'd try. She sucked harder and he pushed deeper inside her mouth.

Red flared behind his eyes and a storm whipped itself into raging life within him. Lost, a sexual haze consuming him, he bolted upright, flipped her over onto her back and dived between her thighs.

Her inner flesh lay plump and pink, a decadent feast he'd never be able to resist. He licked her, again and again then he captured her clit between his lips and rolled his tongue around her. She moaned and sighed then shuddered, her legs trembling and her body convulsing.

No relief. He needed this, to saturate himself in her. Heartbeat pounding, he showered attention on her, until she writhed and cried out, "No more. Come inside me, Tor."

"You can take a little more." He wasn't done yet, not by half. He suctioned his mouth around her hard nipples, first one and then the other and his bear snapped at him, demanding he mark her again. He swept her hair away from her neck, pushed his cock between her legs and barely held his beast back before he plunged deep inside her hot sheath and locked his teeth onto her neck as he did.

"Oh, aye." She urged him on, rocking with him, meeting each and every one of his thrusts. "I need to bite you too."

"Do it." He guided her mouth to his neck, his balls slapping the insides of her thighs as he lunged into her, over and over. "Bite m—"

She sank her teeth into him and her pleasure radiated down their link and swamped his senses. She'd laid claim to him, just as completely as he'd laid claim to him. Her bite was sheer heaven and an aphrodisiac of the greatest sort.

As he blazed toward a precipice of no return, he swiped one finger over her clit below and sent them both soaring from their bodies. Her channel pulsed around him, and his essence spurted deep within the haven of her heat.

"Oh, your bite is sheer perfection." Her channel convulsed around him, squeezing tight, until she slowly settled and drifted on a tide of blissful joy.

Completely spent, he stretched out over top of her, the only woman who'd ever consume him, heart, body and soul, now his to hold for all time. *"There is no other for me, other than you. You're my wife, forever a part of me and now always in my heart."*

"I shall also soon be your very squished wife." She smiled as she gazed at him then gently floated them up, rolled them over and brought them back down onto the furs with him underneath and her on top. She nestled her cheek against his chest and softly sighed. *"I'm sleepy."*

"Then rest." He tucked his arms around her, not prepared to let her move even an inch from him and as her eyelids fluttered down over her cheeks, all pink and flushed, he nabbed the fur he'd discarded, pulled it over them then relaxed and allowed his own exhaustion to take him under. His woman matched him in every way, was all he could ever desire in a mate.

His. Forever his.

Chapter 6

An owl hooted somewhere deep within the encampment's bordering forest and stirred Layla toward wakefulness. She opened her eyes although 'twas still dark outside, the candle within the lamp almost down to the end of its wick. Warmth cocooned her, from her head to the tips of her toes and she stretched, held her breath. Muscles she'd never used before ached, although an ache she fully embraced. Although not so much the ache that demanded she tend to her immediate needs. A spot behind a tree in the forest would do for that.

Wriggling, she tried to free herself from Tor's firm hold. Almost there. She squirmed out and thankfully without waking him, tucked the fur back over top of him and tiptoed to her discarded clothes. She stopped at the sight of Cherub's bag tucked half underneath the pile of furs. The cook had said Cherub had used this tent. She eased the bag out, unbelted the leather flap and flipped the top open. Cherub's clothes lay neatly folded within. She smiled, certain Cherub wouldn't mind in the least if she borrowed some.

From the top, she selected a pale blue riding habit with a lacy cream shirt. She donned the shirt, fastened the skirt at her hips then tugged the jacket on. The sturdy leather boots within the bag would be far more useful than her slippers in traipsing through the woods. With the riding boots on, she took one last look at her deliciously sleeping mate and although she didn't wish to leave him, ducked outside.

A fresh breeze blew in from over the loch and fluttered her hair about, which was likely a complete mess following her night with her mate. Pale colored canvas tents dotted the length of the clearing, the forest rising high behind them while a fire still glowed within the pit in the center of the camp. A good sixty warriors slept around its warmth and two men from amongst their number rose from their bedding, stretched and wandered down toward two warriors on guard at the water's edge.

A glorious loch, private and perfect for her to use lay not far from here, only a short walk through the woods. The loch also sat on their Matheson land and was quite safe, their border patrols always firmly in place between them and their enemy MacKenzie clan.

She set out along the forest trail meandering through the towering pines. Low brush crowded the pathway and she skipped over trailing tree roots in the moonlight before veering off the trail just before the loch. She found the perfect spot and after crouching behind a prickly brushwood, tended to her needs.

Back on the trail, she snuck between two large trunks and halted right before the shimmering waters of a beautiful pool. Small and flawlessly round, the water danced with the reflection of the swaying trees encircling it while high above through the break in the leafy canopy, the stars glittered like diamonds within a peaceful layer of beautiful black.

Along the mossy water's edge, she strolled and passed the odd boulder protruding from the embankment. In a clear spot, she knelt, scooped water and splashed her face then with wet hands, ran her fingers through her hair and tried to tame her golden curls as best as she could.

This loch was so enchanting. She would bring Tor here and

show him this most magical—

A clomp and a rustle sounded within the bordering trees close behind. She held still, her moonlit shadow shimmering over the water and the shadow of another moving in behind her on horseback flickering over hers. Not Tor. For certain. Her mind was still deeply entrenched within his and he slept on. 'Twas likely one of her kin on duty and patrolling this area.

"Well, well. This is a rather fortunate encounter, finding you all alone." Donnan's gravelly voice made the hairs on her arms and neck stand up. Booted feet thumped on the ground and a horse whinnied. "Turn around, Layla."

She pushed to her feet, turned and gasped, clutched a hand to her chest. Blood coated the front of his great plaid and dripped from the dagger he held, the man before her appearing every inch the blood-thirsty warrior he was. "Whose blood is that?" she demanded.

"A hungry wolf. 'Twas either him or me and since I've a great desire to continue living, his life instead came to a fast and sure end."

"Where's Gerald?"

"Gerald is currently tied high within the bow of a tree and unable to get down." Reins in one hand, he tethered his sleek black mount to a low branch, his horse snorting frosty air. He crossed the distance separating them, knelt at the water's edge, dunked his blade in the water then wiped it across the mossy grass and sheathed it at his wrist. The back of his tunic gaped in a diagonal line from one shoulder to his hip, along with a single claw mark scoring his flesh. Blood seeped from the jagged wound.

"You're no' the same man who I spent time with at Dunscaith." He was far more ruthless than he'd ever allowed her to see.

"I'm a warrior, Layla, and you were the one I wanted in my bed. I had a great need to procure a signed betrothal agreement with you, and I did, very successfully at that." He dunked his hands into the water then splashed his face and wiped all trace of the blood from his skin away. "You're also well aware I repudiated my vow when I had no desire to." He rose back to his feet and loomed over her. "Do you wish to make clan MacDonald your enemy?"

"Nay." She shook her head, forced herself to remain standing strong and not show any possible weakness to him. His arrival here was unexpected, yet also expected, which meant she'd been given another chance to make amends, however she could. She certainly wasn't allowing him anywhere near her mate. She'd deal with Donnan on her own this time, her mind connected with Tor's and ensuring she knew exactly where he was. "There must be a way around our current issue, Donnan."

"Only marriage between us will suffice. Your ability is one of the strongest of the battle skills. I want my sons carrying your blood."

"I spoke handfast vows last eve with Tor." She met his gaze, ensured hers remained unwavering. "I will never be your wife."

"Your spirit is strong and rather commendable, although handfast vows can be broken." He narrowed his gaze on her. "Did you consummate those vows?"

"Aye, we did, and I'll never break those handfast vows." She gave him her sternest look to ensure he was left with no doubt of her current intentions, that she would not bow down to him or allow him to hold any sway over her. "You may no' have my fae blood in your line, but you still have the aid of my kind when you go to war, provided you dinnae allow our broken betrothal to cause the alliance between our clans to falter. My father will see things made right. He'll fight at your clan's side, just as he's always done and always will. You'll have lost naught if you but allow it."

"That fact is the only thing keeping me from stealing you

away right this moment."

"No one can force one with my skill to go anywhere we dinnae wish to go." She lifted herself up, swept backward out over the water and hovered beyond his reach.

"Magnificent." He smirked, hands firm on his hips. "I'm no' an ogre or a tyrant, Layla. My temper is fast to rise but I would never have laid a hand on you during our earlier argument. You are safe with me, likely as safe as you are with your warrior, whether you believe it or no'."

"My warrior holds the other half of my soul, just as I hold his. There can be no separating that which will always be destined to be." Now that she'd joined in all ways with Tor, she had a true sense of exactly how deep the bond ran. She'd always known of course, having seen the mated bond taking form between couples within her own clan, but to experience it for herself was something quite different.

"I speak the truth." Frowning, he scrubbed a hand over his whiskered jaw. "My actions during the battle on the beach clearly alarmed you, and for that I humbly apologize. Over the hours since, I've had time to consider all you've spoken of and in truth, I wouldnae wish for a wife who yearned for another. You are right in that regard, although I do demand remedial payment for the broken betrothal. I want a wife who holds fae blood and your father must provide me with another lass in your place. There will be no other satisfaction otherwise. When I leave your land, 'twill be with the fae lass I've wed. A bride for a bride, you could say."

"My father is the one you'll need to speak to on this matter. He is one of Gilleoin's captains, as well as one of the leaders of the village, and he will need to meet with the others to determine if there is a suitable lass for you amongst my fae kind." She hovered back toward him and lowered herself onto the embankment. "Your enemies are still our enemies, the ties between our clans having been in place for an age. Dinnae allow that to falter."

"You are the one who allowed the ties to falter." He slid one callused finger under her chin and slowly leaned in. "I now ask for your aid. Return with me to the keep and stand at my side as I speak to your father."

"I cannae leave my husband behind." Although waking Tor and explaining all she and Donnan had just spoken about would likely rattle him. Tor had already proven he had no tolerance for Donnan, would likely rally against any attempt of negotiation. She'd also been the one to cause this dilemma, and now she'd been given the chance to rectify it, she would. She also needed to ensure the most suitable lasses from the village were chosen for him to pick from, that those lasses were willing to wed him, knew all they needed to know about Donnan before they agreed to speak vows. His bride would certainly need to hold a skill that would allow her to stand strong in her own right alongside him. That she could ensure if she did agree to go and stand at his side as he spoke to Father.

"I willnae have your handfast husband disrupt my upcoming negotiations. We leave now, you and I, and as swiftly as you first brought me here, through the air. The negotiations will take place, and then I'll leave with my bride once she's been chosen, to both my satisfaction and hers."

She couldn't pass this opportunity up. Carefully, she touched her mind to Tor's, found him still blissfully asleep. She nodded at Donnan and gestured toward his horse. "You'll need to leave the horse behind if we're to take the route through the air which you've suggested."

"You have my thanks." He bowed his head in acknowledgement and she lifted them both up, swept them out over the shimmering pool of water then higher still until they soared above the forest's treetops.

With each mile she placed between her and Tor, her heart squeezed tighter. Leaving him hurt, and far more than she'd expected. "Which tree is Gerald restrained within?"

"I managed to persuade him to stop about a half mile from the keep. I'll alert the guards upon our return and they can fetch him, bring him back to the castle."

She'd make sure the guards were alerted as well and not leave it just to Donnan to do.

Once well beyond the sight of the camp's guardsmen patrolling the perimeter of their encampment, she breezed down and across the grassy moors abloom with wildflowers and clumps of purple and pink heather. Along the horizon, a shimmer of red hazed into the lightening blue. 'Twould soon be dawn and the beginning of a new day, one she intended now to make right.

"*Layla?*" Tor stirred and touched her mind. "*Where are you?*"

"*Good morn, my fierce steward.*" The sun breached the horizon and rose higher. She picked up her speed, her hair whipping about her face as she kept her mind partially closed off to him.

"*It would be a good morning if I awoke with you still in my arms, and you haven't answered my question. Where are you?*"

She followed his movements through their merged link. He donned his pants and loose black shirt then slung his war coat studded with bits of steel over top. "*There's been a...development.*"

"*What kind of development?*" With his weapons strapped on, he snuck out of the tent and breathed deep. He followed her scent through the forest toward the loch and prowled the area.

"*Tor, I am no' at the encampment, but on my way back to the castle.*" She couldn't allow him to worry over her. Alongside the stream, she swept then blazed down the trail toward the woods surrounding the castle.

"*Donnan's scent is all over this place and there's blood.*" His low growl rumbled down their link.

"*The blood belongs to a wolf, and Donnan and I have*

spoken. Our broken betrothal is my fault and I must make amends and ensure the alliance between our clans does no' falter. He wishes to speak to Father and if another bride of fae blood can be provided in my place, he'll accept that as satisfaction."

"Damn it, Layla. How could you leave with him when he *made his intentions yesterday so very clear? He wants you as his wife and not another.*" Fury swarmed through from him then fear roared to glaring life. "*Tell me you're all right.*"

"*I'm fine. Truly, I'm fine. I've already informed Donnan that we've spoken handfast vows. He has accepted that we are wed and I will never leave you. He cannae make me. One with my skill isnae so easily restrained.*"

"*Anyone can be restrained. Don't take your eyes off him. I'm coming.*" He was on the move, racing back to camp. He grabbed Tavish from where he sat breaking his fast near the fire and the two of them bounded onto destriers and galloped from the encampment. Tor withheld naught from her, not as she had done with him while he'd slept and guilt consumed her.

"*I'm so sorry.*"

"*Promise me that there'll be no more secrets between us.*"

"*I promise.*" She opened her mind fully to him and a blast of warmth and reassurance flowed through from him. Along with it, he swamped her in his love.

"*We'll get through this, Layla. I'm catching up fast.*"

"*There is naught to worry about. Honestly, I wouldnae have left without you if I'd thought for one moment that there would be any danger in bringing Donnan to my father.*" She was almost home, a peek of the castle showing through the trees ahead.

"Set us down here, Layla." Donnan gestured toward the end of the pine-covered trail as he opened his belted sporran.

She halted at the edge of the forest and gently set them both back down. The House of Clan Matheson rose tall and strong before her and the morning sunshine beamed across the land and lit the fortified stone walls of the keep a glittering gold.

"Raise the portcullis!" The call came from the guardsman standing atop the battlements. The portcullis rose, the clunky sound of its chains reverberating across the outer yard. Horses' hooves pounded then a score of Matheson riders galloped out and rode away from them along the grassy path and up the cliff side trail between their keep and the fae village farther along the loch.

Another group of warriors, all wearing the MacDonald plaid, marched through the gate and strode down to the sea-gate landing where their galley remained moored at the end. MacDonald men on board the galley already busied themselves as if they were preparing to leave. How odd. Searching the sea-gate for one of her clansmen and finding none, she said, "Is there a reason why your men appear—"

Donnan grabbed her, shoved a thick wad of cloth into her mouth from his sporran, jammed a grubby sack over her head then hauled her hands behind her back and shoved her front up hard against the trunk next to them. She fought to move but he snagged twine around her wrists, bound them together. In her ear, he rasped, "I came back here to the keep after stringing Gerald up, told my men to be prepared to leave the moment I returned, hopefully by dawn, then I rode back to the encampment to find you. Surely you didnae think I'd truly ever accept another bride of fae blood, other than you?"

He'd lied, outright lied to her. The bastard.

"There is one thing you need to learn about me, Layla. I never break a vow. I agreed to wed you and I shall." He stroked a finger down her arm and she shivered with disgust.

"I am already wed to Tor," she mumbled through the cloth although her words were almost indistinguishable and damn it, she was now without any sight. She couldn't use her skill if she couldn't see what she needed to move or manipulate. So very few knew exactly how her father's and her skill worked. How had he?

"Loss of sight, loss of skill." He snickered in her ear. "You're surely wondering how I knew. I've always known. My father instructed me well on all he'd discovered over the years having known your father as he did. And by the way, you will repudiate your handfast vow once we reach Dunscaith, and following that, you'll be speaking true marriage vows with me afore a clergyman. 'Twill be those vows alone that shall count and none other." He jerked on her restrained hands, tightened the knots. "I will bed you the moment that is done, then you'll bear my sons who will be as strongly skilled as you are. I will accept no other satisfaction."

"*Tor!*" She screamed his name down their link as Donnan heaved her over his shoulder and her belly thumped into his rock hard shoulder. "*I'm so sorry. I shouldnae have trusted Donnan, nor taken my gaze off him. You must hurry.*"

* * * *

Layla's words echoed through Tor's mind and made his heart stutter as he galloped across the moors toward the castle. He followed her thoughts, picked up that Donnan had shoved a gag in her mouth and blacked out her sight by hooking a sack over her head. Her hands were bound and her belly jolted into Donnan's shoulder with each step Donnan took as he carried her around the forest's edge toward the sea-gate, just out of her Matheson guardsmen's sight. She sensed the fresh breeze coming in off the loch then the crashing of the surf. Heavy footsteps clacked on the stone landing. Donnan's. The rocking of the galley underneath her feet as Donnan set her down then strung her to the center mast and tossed a heavy covering of some sort over her. He tracked each of her movements, and that of their enemy.

Hell, no one would ever hurt or terrorize his mate and get away with it. He gritted his teeth, faced Tavish as they rode. "Layla's in trouble."

"What's happened?" Tavish picked up his pace as he sat low in the saddle, bent his head over his destrier's neck.

"He's blacked out her sight and restrained her, disabled her ability. What she can't see, she can't move. He's now tossed her on board his galley and they're about to set sail. I won't lose my mate." He thrust his knees into his mount's flanks and flew alongside the stream and into the forest. Never had he ridden so hard or so fast. "See if you can reach Julia, Tavish. Alert her to what's happening."

"I'm updating her right now." Tavish grimaced and remained silent as he spoke to his mate along their merged link. With a glance at him, Tavish muttered, "She said Kirk and Cherub left earlier for Stirling to see Gilleoin and Nessa, a flying visit, one they're not expected back from for another hour or two. Julia's alerting the guard and searching for Gregor as we speak."

"Tell them to get down to the sea-gate now. If Donnan sets sail, I'll have a fight on my hands to get my chosen one back." The MacDonald's stronghold on the Isle of Skye was one of the most fortified structures ever constructed and protected by a garrison of hundreds of men. He urged his war horse into a faster pace and whizzed through the forest along the beaten trail. Fallen leaves and pine needles whooshed about the forest floor and he jumped the odd log, ducked his head under a low branch and galloped on. *"Talk to me, Layla."*

"I'm sitting in the hull, roped to the center mast and I can hardly breathe with this gag in my mouth and whatever covering it is they've tossed over me." A wealth of worry channeled through from her. He sensed her pain as she shoved at her bindings and tried to wriggle one hand free. The soft skin of her wrists had almost been rubbed raw from her struggle to free herself. *"Please be careful. I'm surrounded by MacDonald warriors and I have no intention of living on this Earth without you. If you die, then I die."*

"I'm almost there. Tavish spoke to Julia along their link and she's at the castle. She's about to alert the guard and find your father. We're coming, all of us." Determination spurred him on as he hurtled down the final stretch of the trail. He rode hard along the grassy verge of the loch then hauled his mount to a halt a mere horse-head in front of Tavish at the sea-gate landing. He jumped down and sprinted toward the MacDonald galley moored at the end.

Donnan stood at the stern, his claymore drawn and a fierce smirk on his face as one of his men released the mooring rope then bounded on board. They pushed off the landing.

Over his shoulder, he yelled to his brother, "Stay alive, Tavish. It's time to fight."

"I'm right here." Tavish whipped his sword free.

Fight they would. Sword in hand, Tor leapt the distance from the landing to the moving galley, landed in the vessel with Tavish, his blood roaring for revenge and his enemy now standing directly before him. He'd never allow MacDonald to take his chosen one from him. He'd fight, to the death if he must. *"I love you, Layla. Where you are, is where I too shall be, on this Earth or beyond the veil."*

Up along the battlements, the horn trumpeted and he swung and met Donnan's brutal blow while Donnan's men stood at their captain's back and hauled their weapons free.

Chapter 7

Swords clashed and Layla screamed where she sat trussed up to the center mast and unable to see a damn thing. The galley shook and men bellowed. She focused only on Tor and their merged link, his thoughts careening through to her. Strike. Duck. Attack. Donnan and his warriors were coming at him from every side, Tavish the only one aiding him in his fight.

She had to free herself so she could help him. The breeze whispered across her neck under the loose edge of the smelly sack and waves crashed against the side of the galley. She sawed her hands together, the skin at her wrists on fire.

A fierce battle cry boomed all around, then another clash of steel hitting steel rung loud in her ears.

"Hold tight, Layla." Tor's warning ricocheted in her head as the vessel rocked from side to side.

"Get back!" Donnan's shout, his bellow laced with fury. "She's going over."

Over? The galley rolled and she slid down the mast and struck something before her head shattered with pain and the turbulent waters of the bay closed in over her. Within the depths of the icy cold bay, she fought to stay alert and rid herself of her bindings. The underwater rip churned and tossed her about, jerked the sack away into its murky gloom. Goodness. She could finally see, no matter how badly within the darkness of the water.

The ropes attached to the mast pulled excruciatingly tight around her middle. They tore at her chest and legs as they tangled tighter about her. With her skill, she wrenched the bindings free, yanked her hands out then tore the gag from her mouth and clawed for the surface. Her drenched skirts dragged her back down and the swell pulled her even deeper. Nay, the sea wouldn't take her, not now she'd finally found the man who held the other half of her soul. She wanted to live, to have him hold her in his arms and never let her go. "*Tor!*"

"*I'm here.*"

An arm cinched around her waist.

She lurched around and stared into the most piercing golden shifter eyes. Tor firmed his hold on her and pushed them both upward through the twisting current and in a flurry of bubbles, they broke the surface.

"Are you hurt?" She gulped in great drafts of air as she clung to him.

"My heart will never be the same again." He cupped the back of her head and drew her closer. His black hair floated around his neck as he treaded water and kept them both afloat. "Too many of Donnan's men surged to one side during the battle and she went over, fast. I thought I'd lost you. Your thoughts were blaring at me, your struggle mine. I couldn't reach you in time, not through the tangle of sail, ropes, and men."

"You reached me just fine. I'm alive. You're alive, and that's all that matters." She clutched his shirtfront. He was real, his body solid, his flesh warm and his hold exquisitely tight. Next to them, the galley bobbed upside down with its hull on the surface and Donnan's men surging toward the shoreline from the vessel. Donnan led the way, slogged through the surf and onto the beach.

Father stormed toward Donnan, two score of his Matheson warriors flanking him as he bellowed orders and corralled the drenched MacDonald warriors as they stumbled in.

"I'm so sorry I forced you into a battle with Donnan." She looked into his eyes now awash with relief. "I never should have left you, will never do so again."

"All that matters is that you're safe and well." He swept her hair back from her forehead and fingered a spot that throbbed. "You've got a nasty bump that'll bloom into the quite the bruise. Let's get you out of this cold water, warmed up and Donnan and his men dealt with." Holding onto to her, he cut a fast path through the churning waves toward the landing where Tavish stood in soaked battle attire and water sluicing to his feet. Tor gripped her waist and boosted her upward toward his brother.

"Are you well, Layla?" Tavish grasped her, set her on the landing beside him. "Your wrists look red and raw."

"Dinnae worry of them. They'll heal."

Tavish smothered her in a tartan one of her clansmen passed him then offered Tor a hand and heaved him out of the water.

Tor swept her bundled form along the landing and grasped her father's shoulder, one arm still firm around her waist. "Is everyone accounted for?"

"All appear to be here, and thank you for saving my daughter." Father pulled her into a hug. "Julia got word to me of your abduction, but then the galley tipped over afore I could ensure you were set free."

"The sack covering my sight jerked away in the water. I managed to free myself then Tor brought me to the surface. Tor and I spoke handfast vows last eve, Father. Donnan intended for me to repudiate my vow once we reached Dunscaith Castle. He would have forced me to wed him." She hugged her father just as fiercely back. "Donnan also strung Gerald up in a tree a half mile from the keep. You must send someone to free him. This is all my fault and I'm so sorry."

"This is Donnan's doing, no' yours." Father whistled to one his men. "Find Gerald. He'll be in a tree a half mile away."

"Will do." The warrior and another raced to the stables and mounted horses.

"What are we going to do with Donnan and his men?" She rubbed her cheek against Father's arm, his solid presence comforting her just as Tor's fierce warmth and firm hold around her did as well.

"I'll deal with Donnan, although 'tis now because of his rash actions here this very morn that any ties between our clans will now be severed. If we ever ally ourselves with them again, it'll be a very long time away."

Donnan snarled and stormed toward Father, his men rallying in behind him. "Your daughter broke our betrothal agreement and I was simply taking what was rightfully mine."

"My daughter is soul bound to another and none can tear the two apart, no' even I." Father raised his hands, twirled his fingers and with his skill, thrust Donnan toward the landing, right along with his men.

She lifted her own hands toward the overturned galley and with a single flick, she lifted it up. The waters surged and the galley heaved over. Water flowed out of the hull, the ropes and the sail a tangled mess. Wood creaked and groaned as she settled the galley back down at the end of the landing while Father shoved Donnan and his men on board.

"There will be no mingling of fae blood between our clans." Father's voice rose above the din as he glared at Donnan. "Raise arms against me and my kin again and we shall do so with you. Take your men and leave, and never forget that my strength and my daughter's far exceeds yours. None can best those with the 'power of thought.'"

A few of the MacDonald warriors dove into the water and collected their lost oars, boarded and with their men settled on the seats and retrieved oars in hand, rowed out of the bay then heaved their drenched sail up and disappeared across the sea toward Skye.

Relief flared through her. Was it truly over?

"I'm so sorry." She turned in Tor's arms, caught his face in her hands and kissed him, with all the longing and need she harbored for him and he kissed her back, crushing her against his chest.

"It's all over, and no more apologies are needed." He scooped her up and strode toward the forest, leaving Father and her clansmen behind as they made certain Donnan didn't return.

She waved to Father and he lifted a hand in acknowledgment, nodded at her with a gentle smile. Her father would understand Tor's need to get her as far away from Donnan as possible, even though their enemy had now set sail. "Where are we going?"

"To our sacred cavern. I have a fierce need to see with my own eyes that you came to no harm during your abduction, which means I'll be inspecting every single inch of you for injury."

"As long as I too may inspect every single inch of you." She nuzzled his neck, licked over the mark she'd given him then whispered, "I would also like to show you how very truly sorry I am."

"I never want to experience the heart-wrenching fear I did today, ever again." He strode with her up the winding trail, trekked deeper into the forest and marched uphill toward the waterfall and their most precious place. "I also have a desperate need for absolute privacy."

"So do I." She kissed him again, her heart and soul rejoicing at being with him. Aye, absolute privacy they needed, and likely for quite some time.

* * * *

Along the tunnel into their sacred cavern behind the

waterfall, Layla raced with Tor one step behind her. She jumped down onto the boulder wedged under the entrance then bounded onto the soft sand and twirled around. She dropped the tartan she'd been wrapped in and kicked off her riding boots. With her sopping pale blue jacket flung aside, she unfastened the heavy, wet skirts of her riding habit and grinned as Tor shucked his war coat and unbelted his weapons. "I may find taking orders difficult, Tor, but I do intend for you to learn there are plenty of added benefits being mated to me."

"Benefits I intend to claim, each and every one of them."

"The first benefit will be my attention to detail in undressing you." With her mind, she tugged his loose black shirt embroidered with their clan motto on the front pocket free of his faded brown rawhide pants and pulled it over his head. His beautifully broad chest, so heavily muscled and holding a smattering of dark hair, glistened wetly in the sunshine streaming through the wide vent above.

"That's one benefit, I too hold." He stepped closer, traced one finger over her beaded breasts through her lacy cream riding shirt, the fabric so wet the pink of her nipples showed through. "Arms up, my challenging mate."

She lifted them and he swept his hands down her sides, gripped her hem and lifted the shirt up and over her head, her tangled and wet curls plopping onto her back.

"My turn." She levitated him, knelt at his hovering feet and removed his boots then unfastened his pants and stripped them down his muscled legs and off. His cock bobbed free and brushed his belly, rigid and hard and all hers. Needing him now, she swept him out over the steamy heat of their pool and splashed into the warm water after him. Slowly, she lowered him, inch by inch as she stroked over his trim hips and grasped his firm butt. She licked his thickened shaft from root to tip then giggled as he groaned, his feet still nowhere near the sandy floor of the pool as she kept him just where she wanted him.

"Put me down, woman."

"Benefit number two. I can spin you around and do as I wish with you." She slowly twirled him where she stood in the waist-deep water, his feet in the water and his magnificent body on full display, all hard and bulging with muscle. All hers. "My warrior mate."

His golden gaze seared hers as she whirled him back around to face her. "I'm also one warrior who needs to make love to his woman. Set me down so I can, and that's a firm order, one I want you to obey."

"Still terrible with orders, and benefit number three." She giggled again. "Is that I wish only to make love with you and adore every inch of you while I do." She traced the tip of his cock with her tongue and gently palmed his balls in her hand.

He arched into her, his breath whooshing out. "I love how freely you touch me."

"Touching you like this"—she licked all around the head then sucked the salty sweetness that beaded on top—"makes my nipples go hard and heat pool within me below."

"Put me down, now. I need to lick you all over too. I want to taste that pooling heat. It's like sweet honey to my bear and he's ravenous for it."

"Benefit number four." She slowly lowered him, licked up the rigid band of muscles lining his stomach then flicked her fingers over his tiny yet hard male nipples before she sucked on his neck, right over the mark she'd given him last night. Onto her toes, she moved then covered his mouth with hers. She kissed him, until his breathing became as ragged as hers and the sultry warm air around them thickened with a pounding heat. "Is that I'll always be hungry for more of you too."

With his feet now firm on the sandy base of the pool, she lifted herself from the water and gave him exactly what he'd asked for, the ability to lick that pooling heat in her below.

Floating a few inches above the rippling surface, she leaned back, her hair dangling into the water, her back arched over it. "Is this what you wanted?"

"Aye, we'll call this benefit number five, of which shall be offered to me on a daily basis. Your body will be all mine for the taking." He caught her feet, spread her legs and stepped in between her thighs, water splashing his waist. Caressing up her calves and along her inner thighs, he held her pliant with his smoldering gaze alone. "Right now, I'm not sure how slow I can go. I can barely contain my need, or that of my bear's. He's pushing for more of you, so hungry to hold you and completely determined to never let you go. As am I."

"Benefit number six. I freely give you all of me. I always will, so go as fast or as slow as you like. We have no need to leave this sacred place anytime soon."

"I love how you think." He stroked over her hips, up her sides and cupped her breasts then with his thumbs swiping the tips, he bent his head between her thighs and licked her folds. He groaned, pulled back a touch, brushed his nose against her nub and breathed deep. With pure need lacing his tone, he rumbled, "Your scent is the sweetest yet wildest I've ever encountered. I want to smother myself in it."

"I would never stop you if that's what you wished to do."

"Good answer." He plunged one finger inside her and imbibed at the very heart of her, his tongue moving so seductively, so sensually across her flesh.

Desire for more swarmed through her and she widened her legs farther and gasped as he loved her with such heart-racing passion. Consumed by his perfect touch, she soared to such a fierce height until she couldn't contain her need a moment longer. She cried out his name, "Tor, I want you inside me."

"Bring yourself down or lift me up."

"I'm coming." She pushed herself up with her skill, hooked her arms around his neck, slid down his wet body and impaled herself on top of him, his cock spearing through her folds. She moaned her delight, rubbed her breasts against his chest and reveled in their fast joining.

"Bite me, now." He gripped her bottom and plunged into her, over and over and she scraped her teeth back and forth along his neck although before she could bite him, he sank his teeth into her neck and sent her flying to the stars. Her inner muscles clamped down on him and she soared, bright lights bursting in a myriad of beautiful rainbow colors all around.

"More." Teeth firm, she bit him and he shuddered, groaned and thrust even harder inside her. Untold pleasure radiated through her as she met each and every one of his hard and fast strokes, and as she urged him even deeper, she catapulted from her body a second time, her second orgasm roaring swiftly through her, hard on the heels of her first. *I love you, Tor, with all my heart and soul. You are my everything and all.*

"I love you too, and from this moment forth, no one will ever separate us again." He plunged balls-deep inside her, his seed shooting in one hot rush straight to her core.

Kissing him, she reveled in their joining, in being as one with the only man she'd ever live for. He held not only the other half of her soul, but her very heart in his hands, one that would forever beat for him. Only him.

For all time.

* * * *

Tor came with such a wildly desperate need as Layla gripped his cock and pulled him ever deeper inside her. She continued to pulse, her heavenly heat his home and her heart and soul his to hold on to for all time.

She moaned in his arms, soft murmurs that kept his cock hard even though he'd just come. Hell, he still needed her, and with a deep thirst that would never be quenched.

Kissing her, he delved into the honeyed recesses of her mouth, cupped her lushly curved bottom and walked with her in his arms though the water toward the overhanging ledge at the edge of the pool. Gently, he laid her down on the thick slab of stone, gripped the edge and hauled himself up beside her, water sluicing down his body.

"I can read your thoughts and you appear to need more." She held out her hands for him and he went to her, laid down over top of her sensuously delicious body.

"A lifetime with you will never be enough." He swept his tongue inside her mouth, the need to touch all of her riding him hard. This time when they came together, he intended to trace every inch of her smooth skin with his hands and tongue, to show her with his dedicated touch just how very much he loved her. Reveling in the sight of all her creamy flesh, he palmed the fullness of her breasts, licked then sucked her nipples deep inside his mouth, first one and then the other. He gorged himself on her, until her wild cherry scent swirled in and around his senses and drove him completely mad. "I'm going to eat you."

"As you wish." She feasted her gaze on him, roamed across his chest and down to his throbbing cock. "I'm fairly hungry myself. I barely got a taste of you afore. May I?"

"Later." A sizzling pressure burned at the base of his spine and flared all the way around to his cock. His shaft lengthened and hardened to a staggering degree. "Much later. It's time for my bear to have his way." He rolled her onto her belly, slid one arm underneath her waist and lifted her up onto her hands and knees. "And this is how he wants you."

"Aye, please. This is how I want you too." She wriggled her luscious bottom, her glorious golden hair sliding wetly off her back and sweeping the ledge as she peered over her shoulder at him.

"I need to bite you again." He rubbed his nose against the small of her back, nipped her skin then crawled in over top of her, the silky wetness of her body making his bear rumble with pleasure at being able to slide against all her smooth flesh. Head dipped, he razzed his teeth back and forth over the sensitive skin of her neck then whispered, "Are you ready?"

"I'll always be ready." Stretching, she offered the long column of her creamy flesh to him and he licked her skin, sucked it deep inside his mouth, swept one hand down her side and trailed his fingers through her golden curls below. He fondled her clit, moaned with greedy need as she arched back into him, her breasts swaying beneath her and brushing his arm.

"Tell me what you want, my love."

"For you to join us together as one." She reached underneath her, slid her fingers around his shaft and rubbed the head of his cock over her drenched folds and coated him in her heavenly scent.

"We are going to need one very long honeymoon, just the two of us, all alone, right here."

"Aye, I'd love such a honeymoon." She pushed her backside into his groin and he thrust his cock inside her, pulled back then pushed all the way back inside her again. She lifted up and rocked with him and as she did, he rubbed her clit and plunged even deeper. She met each of his fierce moves with such exquisite precision, his balls slapping the insides of her thighs and sending him half crazed. Unable to halt himself, he growled and bit down on her neck.

She screamed, her inner muscles clamping around him and squeezing him with such sheer perfection. She flew right over the edge and he soared right along with her, her body bathing him in her glorious heat and her channel clenching so beautifully around him.

Never had he felt so completely whole, as if the woman in his arms had finally gifted him with the rest of who he was. Without her, he would never survive, and of that he had no doubt.

As Layla went limp in his arms, he gently lowered her down onto the ledge on her belly and curled his body around hers, the steamy heat of their cavern enveloping them. He nibbled on the side of her neck, his heart and soul in paradise and when she sighed, so dreamily, he grinned and only wished to hear her sigh that way all over again.

Aye, he was home, right here with his mate, the only one who could ever satisfy both him and his bear. She was the most precious gift, a treasure he'd cherish for the rest of his days.

Always and forever.

Chapter 8

In her chamber on the second floor of the castle, Layla snuggled in bed with her warrior shifter and smiled as happiness burst inside her. It had been three weeks since Donnan had been sent winging back toward Skye and she and Tor had reunited within their sacred cavern. Three weeks of wedded bliss and enjoying all the benefits of their mated bond.

"We need to move and get dressed if we want to make it to our own wedding celebration. No more handfast wife for me, you'll be my wife in truth within a matter of hours." Tor rubbed his chest against her breasts as he caressed her bare back. Father John from the priory had arrived the day before and she could barely contain her excitement at finally being able to speak vows with her mate before their entire clan.

"I have something I must speak to you about first." She caught his hand, pressed a kiss against the warmth of his palm. Her ring blazed from her finger, the large stone set atop a band of gold the same gorgeous golden color as her mate's stunning shifter eyes. After a sneaky trip back to his time with Cherub, he'd returned with this ring, lowered to one knee and reaffirmed his oath to her. Never had she seen such an extravagant or more beautiful piece of jewelry, or been so filled with love. She'd accepted his ring then ensured she shared every single benefit to being mated to her brought him.

"Then speak. No more secrets between us, remember?"

"I remember, and this is less of a secret and more like a hopeful feeling. My courses are late, should have arrived four or five days ago. I know that does no' sound like long, but I'm never late."

"You're saying you might be expecting?" He tipped her onto her back, flicked the bed sheet covering them away and caressed her belly, the sunshine beaming through her window playing across his bare skin and hers. "Let me check."

"Pardon?"

"My shifter kind can scent when our mate is at her most fertile and then again when she has conceived." He shuffled down, rubbed one cheek over her flat belly and breathed deep. With a rumbling growl, he scented the air then grinned. "Mmm, you smell incredible. Like wild cherries and something else. I'm picking up a new aroma, one which can only signify one thing."

She pushed up, shoved him onto his back and straddled his hips as she sat on top of him. Jiggling up and down, she giggled. "Tell me exactly what that new aroma signifies."

"That you're carrying my child." He edged up onto his elbows and licked the beading tips of her breasts swaying so close to his mouth. "My brother and parents and my entire clan are going to be ecstatic when they hear the news."

"My father too will be over the moon." Never had she ever expected to be gifted with such a fiercely loving and loyal mate, and now a babe all of her own. With her thoughts open to his, she shared all the wonderful new emotions rolling through her and he sent his love and happiness flowing right back.

"I believe this news deserves a celebration like no other." His devious grin spoke of exactly what kind of celebration, one she heartily desired too. "Benefit number five will be required this very minute, my love. Your body will be all mine for the taking."

"As you wish. I freely give you all of me." She rubbed against his cock rising eagerly against her entrance. "Let us celebrate this new adventure we're about to embark on."

"An adventure I can't wait to undertake." He cupped the back of her head and drew her mouth to his. Kissing her, so intimately and so passionately, he made her tremble until she was an achy, hungry mess.

"Never let go of me." She guided his shaft to her entrance and sank down on him. At the heart of her, he now belonged and nowhere else.

"You are my wife, my lover, the other half of my soul." With one powerful stroke, he thrust deep, their souls completely entwined as they soared to the heavens.

Ahead of her, she had a lifetime of loving her mate, and between his future time and hers here, she most certainly would. No one would ever separate them again.

Their two hearts now beat as one, and their love for each other, rose to the very heavens themselves.

Sweet love. It would be theirs forever.

Catch the next book in this tantalizing series.
Highlander's Sword, Book Six.

Author's Note

Clan Matheson descends from a twelfth century man called Gilleoin, a man who was believed to have been from the ancient Royal House of Lorne. The name Matheson has been attributed to the Gaelic words Mic Mhathghamhuim which means "Son of the Bear," and the clan chief's arms carry two bears as supporters. In the twelfth century, clan Matheson settled around the area of Loch Alsh, Loch Carron, and Kintail, and gave their allegiance to clan MacDonald whose chiefs were the Lords of the Isles. Clan Matheson became a large and powerful clan with a force of around two-thousand men, although by the middle of the sixteenth century they'd diminished greatly in size and influence due to the blood feuds raging across the isles at that time. This warring left them to possess less than a third of the original Matheson property on Loch Alsh.

I've made mention in this story of Dunscaith Castle, the stronghold of clan MacDonald on the Isle of Skye. Dunscaith Castle was first known as "Dun Sgathaich" and has strong ties to the heroes and heroines of Celtic legend. The castle itself is named after the legendary Scottish warrior woman Sgathaich, a great teacher of the martial arts, and arts of combat. Dunscaith Castle sits at the mouth of Loch Eishort and dates back to the early 1300s, although a castle or fortification of some type has in fact occupied this site from a far earlier date. For the purposes of this story, I've kept that earlier dated stronghold's name as Dunscaith Castle to better describe the location's setting for clan MacDonald in this era of the 1200s I've written within.

It's time for the whispers to reignite. Clan Matheson are the "Son of the Bear."

This story is woven with as much accuracy to the period and locations as possible, although any mistakes made are mine alone.

Please feel free to search for any of my other works. I simply adore strong heroines, and have a ton of fun matching them with their honorable alpha heroes.

Looking for more sexy Scottish adventure?

Catch a teaser excerpt of the next book in
The Matheson Brothers series.

Highlander's Sword

The Matheson Brothers, Book Six

by Joanne Wadsworth

Highlander's Sword

The Matheson Brothers, Book Six

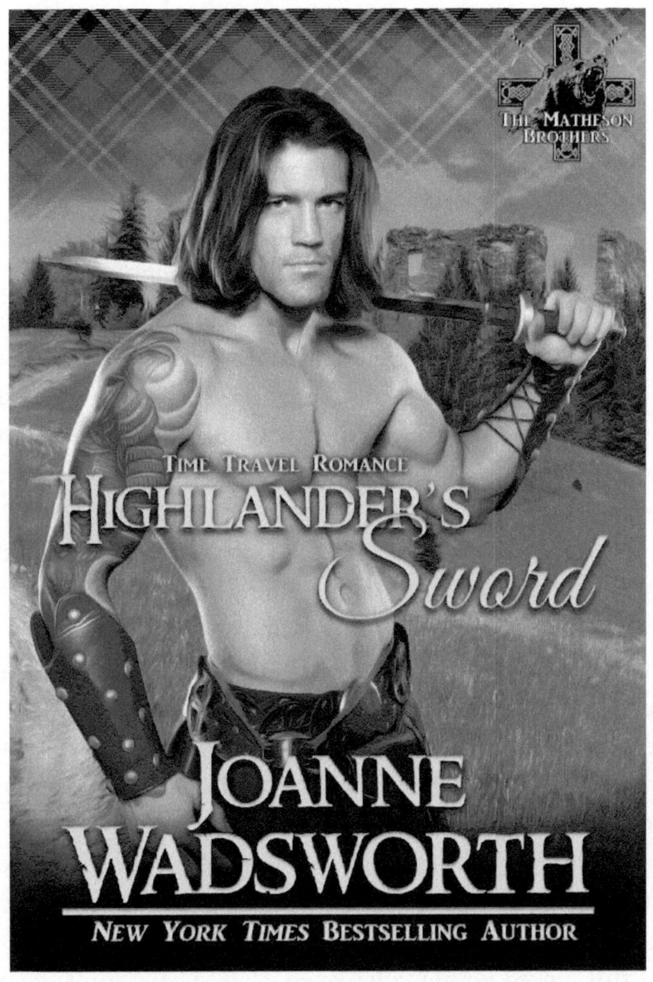

Teaser Excerpt

Up the stairs to the battlements, Alec bolted then stopped behind the woman who had every hair on his neck rising. He breathed deep, drew in Annella's intriguing fragrance, one that held the golden and glittery enchantment of a night sky teeming with stars. Her scent evoked the dream realm she traveled within, and made his lower region harden with lust. She stared up at the blood moon as if it intrigued her, her long golden tresses fluttering in the breeze and whispering over his arms and chest. Hell, she was so small of stature, the sword belted at her side all that gave any indication she in fact knew how to battle.

Carefully, he spread his hands over her hips, then determined to prove his point, that she wasn't his chosen one, he muttered, "Those who are soul bound can never harm the other, but all I want to do right now is sink my claws into you and rip you apart. You need to steer well clear of me, to leave and never return."

"Since the night we met"—she turned in his embrace and he retracted his claws for fear he'd actually scratch her—"you've grumped and growled and snapped at me to be gone, but through it all I still sensed within you a deep need to have someone close. I am here if you wish to talk, can provide quite the listening ear if you were but prepared to accept me. We are meant to be together. A bond certainly wouldnae have formed between us otherwise."

"I'm a warrior, born and bred. I fight, draw blood and have no issue doing so." It would take only one wrong move on his part and he could so easily kill her. Why couldn't she see that? "I fight within my clan's specialist team who work high level government cases, and out of all my kin, I'm the one who gets called away from Ivanson Castle the most. My beast isn't just aggressive, he's bloodthirsty, which makes him the perfect assassin when needed to take down the vilest of criminals."

"I've chased a few vile criminals myself." She dissolved into a wisp and swirled around then reemerged behind him with her sword in hand. She tapped the tip of her blade against his belted sword. "Arm yourself and train with me for what remains of this night. I must be fully prepared to fight Duncan MacKenzie when I find him. I cannae lose my coming battle with him if I wish to free my father and brother."

"You shouldn't be fighting anyone on your own, and certainly not a warrior who managed to capture both of your closest kin." He lunged, grasped her sword hand, his fingers sliding through nothing but air as she wisped back farther and reappeared.

"Nay, you willnae catch me out that easily, my mighty bear."

"I'm not your damn mighty bear."

"Please, that is no way to talk to a woman, and your chosen one at that." With a wink, she wagged a finger at him, her royal blue tunic cinched in at her tiny waist with a golden tasseled belt that swayed to her knees as she moved. Her black breeches, of the softest rawhide, molded her legs, while her pert backside wiggled as she moved.

"I don't see you as a woman, but as a lethal opponent."

"Then raise your blade."

"Training with me is a very bad idea." Still, he slid his sword free of his scabbard and rocked from foot to foot, his beast always prepared for any form of fighting. Perhaps if he trained with her then she'd realize how dangerous he was, leave then hopefully never come back. It was a plan at least. He'd grump and growl a whole lot more as he battled with her, make sure she understood just how fierce and grizzly he could get. That should scare her away.

The Matheson Brothers

Highlander's Desire, Book One
Highlander's Passion, Book Two
Highlander's Seduction, Book Three

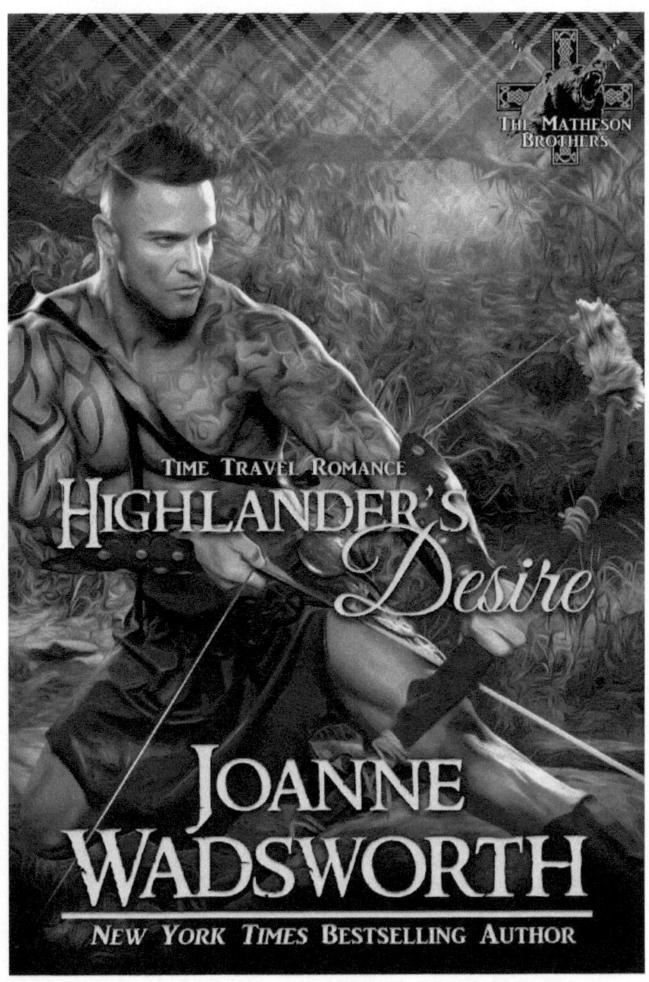

The Matheson Brothers Continued

Highlander's Bride, Book Seven
Highlander's Caress, Book Eight
Highlander's Touch, Book Nine

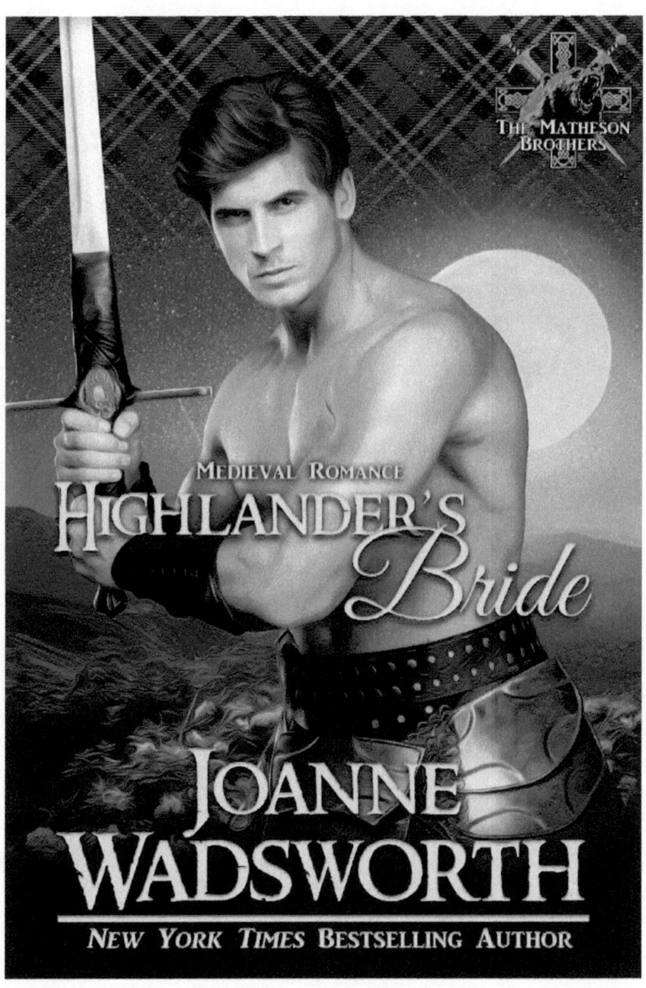

The Matheson Brothers Continued

Highlander's Shifter, Book Ten
Highlander's Claim, Book Eleven
Highlander's Courage, Book Twelve
Highlander's Mermaid, Book Thirteen

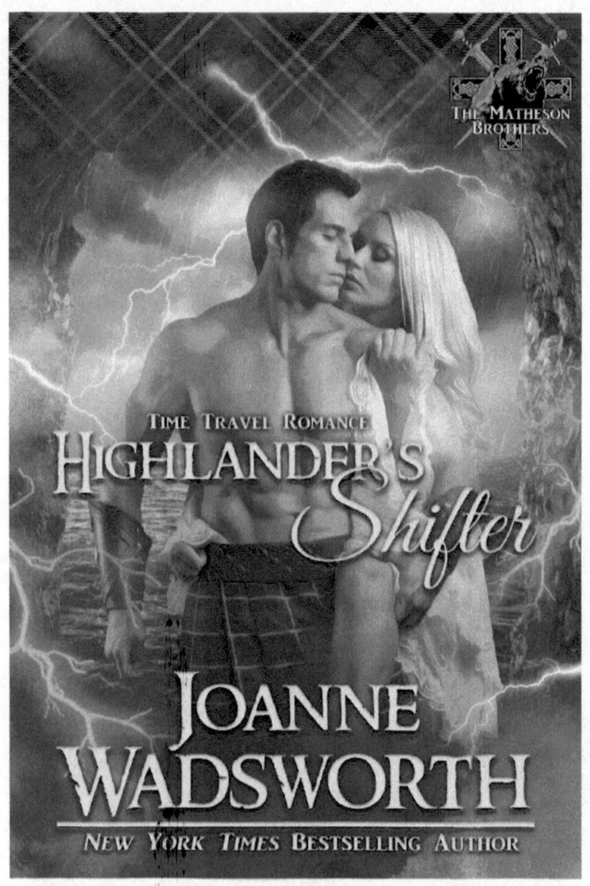

Highlander Heat

Highlander's Castle, Book One
Highlander's Magic, Book Two
Highlander's Charm, Book Three
Highlander's Guardian, Book Four
Highlander's Faerie, Book Five
Highlander's Champion, Book Six

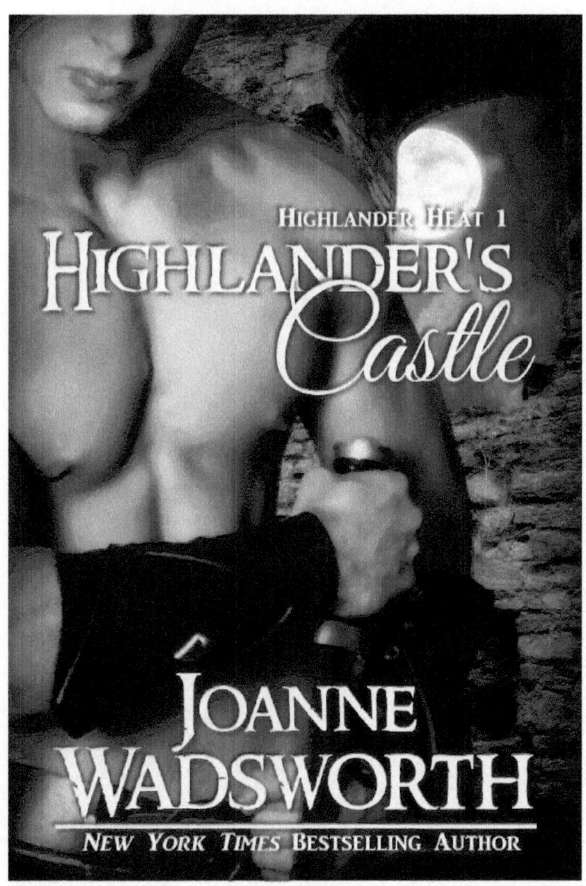

JOANNE WADSWORTH

Regency Brides

The Duke's Bride, Book One
The Earl's Bride, Book Two
The Wartime Bride, Book Three
The Earl's Secret Bride, Book Four
The Prince's Bride, Book Five
Her Pirate Prince, Book Six

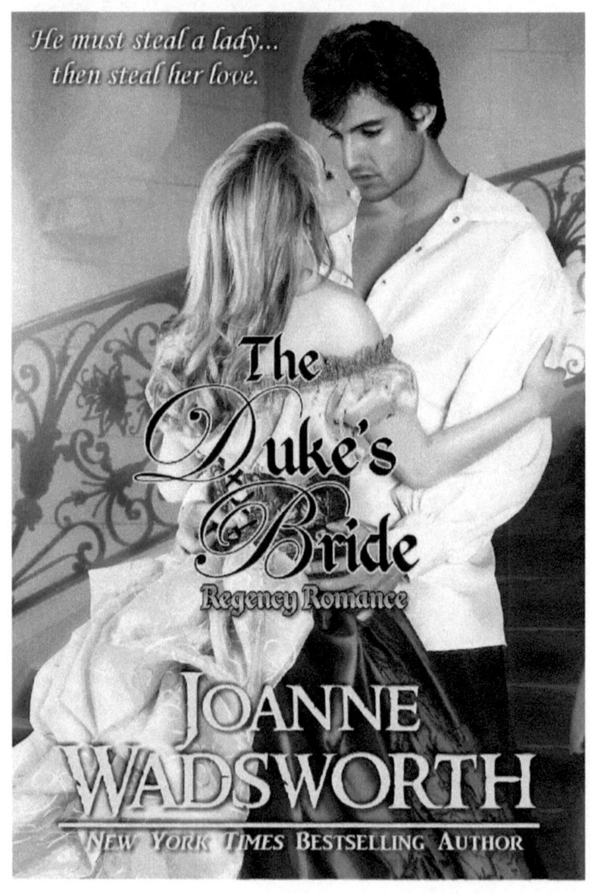

Princesses of Myth

Protector, Book One
Warrior, Book Two
Hunter (Short Story - Included in Warrior, Book Two)
Enchanter, Book Three
Healer, Book Four
Chaser, Book Five

Billionaire Bodyguards

Billionaire Bodyguard Attraction, Book One
Billionaire Bodyguard Boss, Book Two
Billionaire Bodyguard Fling, Book Three

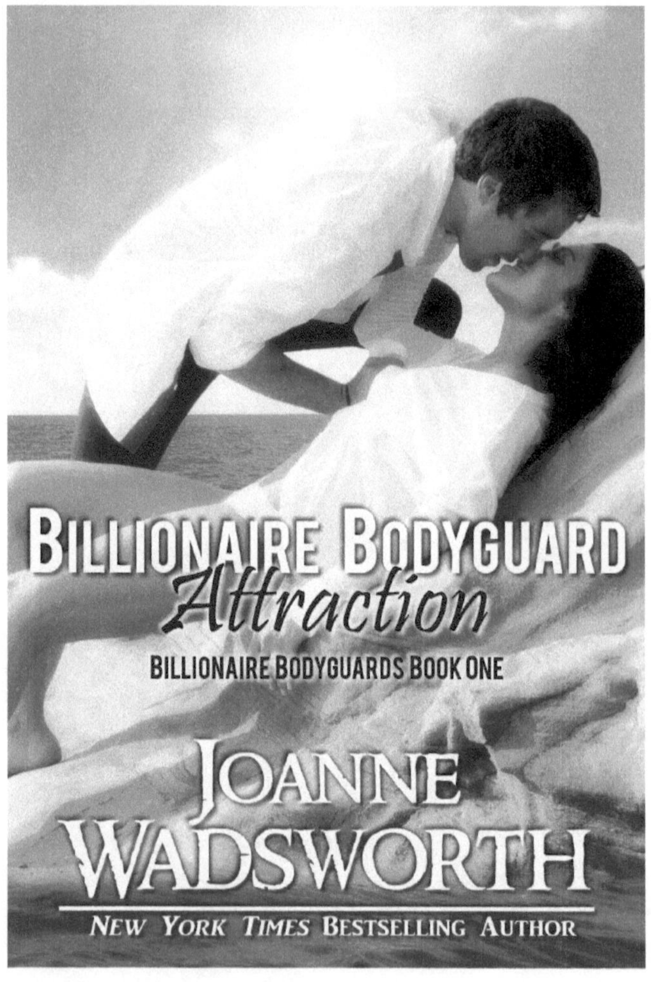

JOANNE WADSWORTH

Joanne Wadsworth is a *New York Times* and *USA Today* Bestselling Author who adores getting lost in the world of romance, no matter what era in time that might be. Hot alpha Highlanders hound her, demanding their stories are told and she's devoted to ensuring they meet their match, whether that be with a feisty lass from the present or far in the past.

Living on a tiny island at the bottom of the world, she calls New Zealand home. Big-dreamer, hoarder of chocolate, and addicted to juicy watermelons since the age of five, she chases after her four energetic children and has her own hunky hubby on the side.

So come and join in all the fun, because this kiwi girl promises to give you her "Hot-Highlander" oath, to bring you a heart-pounding, sexy adventure from the moment you turn the first page. This is where romance meets fantasy and adventure…

To learn more about Joanne and her works, visit
http://www.joannewadsworth.com